Magical Moon Cat

"Look, leave me alone, will you?" Conrad
burst out. "If you want to know, I asked my
parents if I could have a puppy last night.
They said no way! I can't have a kitten or a
rabbit or a guinea pig. I can't have a pet full
stop, because my little brother is allergic! Are
you happy now?"

Magical Moon Cat

Moonbeans and the Circus of Wishes

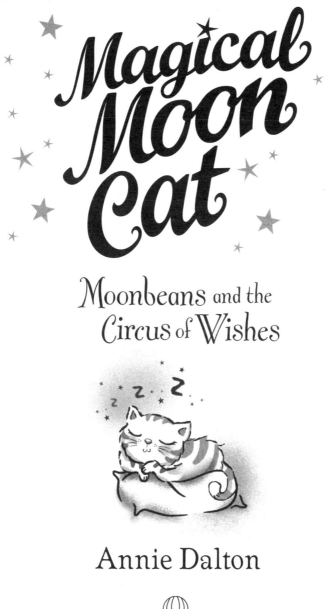

Annie Dalton

USBORNE

For Megan and Grace

First published in 2012 by Usborne Publishing Ltd., Usborne House, 83-85 Saffron Hill, London EC1N 8RT, England. www.usborne.com

Text copyright © Annie Dalton, 2012 Cover illustration by Tuesday Mourning. Inside illustrations by Katie Lovell. Illustration copyright © Usborne Publishing Ltd, 2012

The right of Annie Dalton to be identified as the author of this work has been asserted by her in accordance with the Copyright, Designs and Patents Act, 1988.

The name Usborne and the devices are Trade Marks of Usborne Publishing Ltd.

A CIP catalogue record for this book is available from the British Library.

ISBN 9781409526346 00490/1
JFMAM JASOND/12

Printed in Dongguan, Guangdong, China.

Contents

Spangle, the circus horse

1

"What's your best thing so far?" Jax asked her friend Howard.

Jax and her friends were in the visitors' café at the Goose Green City Farm, hungrily munching burgers and chips. Outside it was a sunny but wildly windy day, which Jax thought was completely perfect weather for a class trip. As she watched, an autumn leaf flattened itself against the window of the café, then went whirling away across the farmyard.

Howard was still thinking about his best thing. "Probably the sheepdogs," he said at last.

"They were cool."

"They were my best too," said Lilia, who liked to agree with people. "And the cute little lambs."

"Their jaws were like nutcrackers though!" Conrad said with a grin. "Mine almost pulled the feeding bottle right out of my hand!"

As usual, Conrad's voice was twice as loud as anyone else's in the café and their teacher gave him a sharp look. Conrad was the cheekiest boy in the school. He even *looked* cheeky, with his spiky ginger hair sticking up above his friendly freckled face. These days he was one of Jax's best friends, though it hadn't always been that way.

Watching Conrad and the others chatting enthusiastically about their morning at the City

8

Farm, Jax felt a twinge of sadness go through her. *I wish Moonbeans was here*, she thought. She hadn't brought him because she knew that taking a magical moon kitten on a class trip – even if he faithfully promised to stay invisible – was just asking for trouble.

Some of Moonbeans's magic must have rubbed off on her though, because the City Farm cat had been following Jax around all

morning! He was called  Bandit and he had a piratical black patch over one eye, and had absolutely refused to let Jax out of his sight.

"I think he can smell my cat, Beans," Jax had explained shyly to the City Farm helpers, Simon and Nan. *Can he smell that Beans is from a totally different world though?* she'd wondered.

Jax was the only human in Goose Green who knew Moonbeans was from a magical alien planet, but animals always seemed to guess straight away.

At this moment, Bandit was outside the café, mewing and trying to get in every time a visitor opened the door. "Are you sure you haven't got magical powers?" Nan asked Jax, laughing as she firmly closed the door on him.

Jax nervously laughed back, but she was thinking that magic sometimes made life *really* complicated.

A rude noise surprised her out of her thoughts, but it was only Conrad, squirting extra ketchup on his burger from an almost empty plastic bottle. This earned him another sharp look from their teacher, but Conrad didn't seem to notice.

"This farm is *ace!*" he said enthusiastically.

"I didn't really believe anyone could squeeze an actual farm inside a busy city, did you?"

"Not unless it was like a little *dollies'* farm!" Ruby-Rose giggled, twirling one of her curly bunches. Though she had completely stopped being a child star these days, Ruby-Rose still went in for child-star hairstyles. Today her bunches were tied up with shiny yellow ribbons that were pulled so tight, Jax was sure they must be giving her a headache!

"I really loved those sheepdogs," Conrad said wistfully. "I wish I could have a dog – or any kind of animal really."

"Isn't it your birthday soon?" Jax said. "You could ask your mum and dad for a puppy."

His face lit up. "I might do that." Then his

eyes clouded again. "But they'll probably say no!"

"Why would they say no?" asked Howard.

"His little brother's got allergies," explained Ruby-Rose.

Conrad looked dejected for a moment, then he noticed Ruby-Rose putting down her knife and fork. "Don't you want those chips, Ruby?" he asked hopefully.

"No, you can have them if you want them." She pushed her plate over.

"My mum calls me the human dustbin!" Conrad was already squirting on more ketchup.

"Your mum's got a point," Lilia agreed, giggling.

After lunch, Jax's class went back out into the farmyard, where Nan and Simon were waiting.

The helpers both wore faded jeans, muddy boots, and sweatshirts that said *Goose Green City Farm*. Neither of them looked anything like the country farmers Jax had seen on TV. Simon had long dreadlocks and Nan had pink spiked hair and a stud in her nose.

"We've got a surprise for you," Nan said with a grin.

When the children saw the huge horses harnessed to two old-fashioned carts, their eyes grew wide.

"They're shire horses," Simon explained. "In the old days they did the work that was too heavy for smaller horses, pulling ploughs or heavy loads. See those huge, fluffy feet? Like they're wearing ankle boots? All shire horses have those."

The nearest horse nosed hopefully at Conrad's school blazer.

"This is Punch."
Nan produced a
windfall apple
from her pocket.
"You can give this
to him if you want
– just keep your
hand completely flat."

"Conrad, *don't!*" Lilia gasped. "His teeth are like *railings!*"

Conrad shook his head. "Punch won't hurt me." He held out Nan's apple on the flat of his hand. With incredible gentleness, the horse took it, then began to crunch with its supersized teeth.

"You're good with animals," Nan said. "Punch trusts you."

Conrad went bright red but Jax knew he was pleased.

"Now, half the class will be coming with me," said Simon, smiling. "And the rest will go with Nan."

Jax and her friends ended up in Nan's cart, pulled by Punch. Nan jumped into the driver's seat. "Walk on!" she told Punch.

"I feel like someone in the olden days, don't you, Jax?" Lilia whispered as their cart moved out of the farmyard after Simon's, pulled by the sedately trotting shire horse.

"I do actually," Jax agreed. Perched comfortably among the hay bales with all her friends, she thought this was the perfect way to see the farm.

Bandit had immediately hopped up into the cart with them. Now he was sitting beside his new best friend, Jax, staring intensely into her eyes, and making husky chirruping sounds, almost like he was asking her a question.

If Moonbeans was here, he'd know what Bandit was saying, Jax thought. *Actually he'd know what all the animals were saying.* It would be so cool, she thought, to know what animals talked about amongst themselves!

"I thought pigs were just plain pink," said Conrad suddenly. "You've got brown pigs and pigs with spots." They were passing an orchard where pigs were happily rooting around among the fallen apples.

"Our pigs all belong to old-fashioned breeds," Simon explained. "That's one reason we set up the City Farm – to help protect rare breeds."

Jax was dreamily looking around her. She still thought it was strange to see farm animals grazing with tower blocks looming in the background.

Nan made Punch stop beside a paddock

where an elderly piebald pony stood nose-to-nose with an equally elderly donkey.

The pony immediately trotted over to make friends.

"This is Spangle," Nan told them. "She's retired now, but she's had a really unusual life. She used to be part of a travelling circus!"

"Can she do tricks?" Lilia wanted to know.

"She can do loads of tricks!" Nan said. "She can actually do sums! The ringmaster would ask her to add two and two, or take five away from ten, and Spangle would knock her hooves on the ground to tell him the answer."

"How come she's not with the circus now?" asked Bella, one of Jax's classmates.

"These days most circuses have moved on from using performing animals," Nan explained. "Spangle's owners asked us if we'd give her a permanent home here on the City Farm."

But Jax saw the circus pony's wistful expression as the children drove away, and she didn't need a magic moon cat to tell her what Spangle was thinking. Probably some animals disliked being forced to perform, but Spangle actually seemed to miss all the excitement.

They drove around the farm in a big circle, following Simon's cart all the way. Then, on the home stretch, Nan clicked her tongue to make Punch go faster and they suddenly went speeding past the others and back into the farmyard, to loud cheers from Jax and her friends.

Jumping down from the cart, Nan went to

fling open a door to one of the barns. "I think you're going to like what's in here," she said with a grin.

The children followed her into the barn and everyone said, "Ahh!"

A litter of little Border collie puppies tumbled and wrestled around her, while their mother looked on, her tail wagging.

There were other small animals in the barn too: lop-eared rabbits, guinea pigs, and a mother goat with her kids. But Conrad only had eyes for the puppies. He immediately got down in the straw with them, letting them climb all over him. "Check this little dude!" he told Jax. "He's got white ankle socks, look!"

"Conrad, did you just sniff his paws?" Ruby-Rose said, giggling.

He nodded, his eyes shining. "They smell like toast and peanut butter. Go on, smell them!"

Ruby-Rose just shook her head, still laughing. "No, thanks!"

Bandit seemed totally unimpressed by the puppies, Jax noticed. If they got too close, he boxed them sharply with his paws, then went back to rubbing lovingly against Jax's ankles.

"You're a cat magnet and Conrad is a dog magnet," Lilia told Jax.

"Conrad isn't a dog magnet," said Howard. "He's an *animal* magnet."

It was true. When Conrad left the puppies  to look at the goats, all the little kids immediately rushed at him, bleating and sticking inquisitive noses in his pockets. Surrounded by bouncy baby goats, Conrad broke into a beaming smile. "This is the best day of my whole life," he told everyone.

Nan hastily stopped the littlest kid from eating Conrad's jumper. "You don't want to go home to your mum in just your underwear!" she warned him with a laugh. "Goats will eat anything."

"Just like Conrad!" Ruby-Rose teased.

"Be fair, I don't eat wool!" he said, grinning.

Then, quite suddenly, their day at the City Farm was over.

"Sorry, guys, but it's home time now. We've got to round up the cows and put them in their stalls for the night," Nan explained.

Conrad didn't say anything, but Jax saw his smile fade.

"We're trying to raise the funds to pay for

another full-time worker," Simon told the children. "Until then, we have to rely on volunteers. We badly need more people to come forward."

Nan nodded. "Maybe you could help us spread the word? Tell your friends at school and everyone else you know all about us, then we might get more local people volunteering to help on the farm."

Jax immediately made up her mind that she was going to tell everybody who came into Mum's café about the City Farm!

"We've got some freebies before you go!" Simon said, and he and Nan started handing out souvenir caps and badges.

As Jax took her seat on the coach, everyone was chatting excitedly about their day out. Only Conrad, normally the noisiest boy in the school, didn't say a word. She heard Ruby-Rose say, "Didn't you get a cap, then, Conrad?"

Conrad snapped, "It's in my pocket, all right! Why do you care if I wear my stupid cap?"

When their coach had dropped them off in the playground, Conrad went running towards the infant school without a word to anyone.

"What's up with him?" said Jax.

"Conrad has to collect his little brothers when his mum's at work," Lilia explained.

"I know that," Jax said, frowning. Conrad had been walking his little brothers back from school ever since his big brother, Lenny, left home. "But he doesn't usually rush off without saying goodbye."

"He seems really upset about something," said Ruby-Rose.

"What, though?" Jax said, puzzled. "At the farm, he said this was the happiest day of his life."

"That could actually be quite upsetting," Howard suggested gently. "You know, if this was the happiest day of your life, then – *bosh* – suddenly it's over."

Jax watched Conrad disappear into the school. *I'm so lucky*, she thought. *I'm the luckiest person I know.* Since Moonbeans came, she'd never had to worry that one day her happiness might run out. When you live with a moon cat, every day is magical and new.

Out of all the children on Planet Earth, Jax had been picked to be Moonbeans's special human; and now he was at home, waiting.

Moonbeans has a dream

2

Jax waited impatiently for the green man to appear, then she hurried over the crossing.

"See ya, wouldn't want to be ya!" Lilia sang out after her. Jax waved to her friend from the other side of the road, then went racing down the street towards her mum's café.

Outside the Red Hot Wok, her mum's friend, Mei Lee, was putting up a new menu. She smiled at Jax. "Hi, Ellie Mae! Isn't it windy today? Winter will soon be here."

"It's Halloween first," said Jax breathlessly.

"Oh, yes, trick or treat!" said Mei Lee. "I must buy a pumpkin to put in the window!"

Jax could see the café now, its sign swinging in the wind. The first time Jax had set eyes on Dolly's Diner, as the café used to be called, she thought her mum had made the biggest mistake of her life. But in a few short weeks, Laura Jackson had turned the scruffy inner-city diner into the most popular café in Goose Green. It was true that she'd had a little magical help from Moonbeans, but only Jax and Beans knew about that!

Jax still felt a tingle of magic go through her every time she read the café's new name on the brightly-coloured sign: *The Dream Café*.

It was funny to think that her mum genuinely believed the name was all her own idea. But of course, there was no way Mum would ever imagine that the café had been renamed by mysterious extraterrestrials, who Beans simply referred to as the Aunts. Beans said they were incredibly ancient beings, older than the stars, who had always taken a kindly interest in Planet Earth.

It was the Aunts who'd sent Moonbeans to live with Jax above the café, as part of their daring and ambitious plan for Goose Green. To the Aunts, the Dream Café was more than just a place to chat over coffee and cupcakes. It was a place where dreams could come true.

Jax opened the door and a flurry of autumn leaves followed her inside. Moonbeans must have recently passed through, because the air was softly pink and shimmery in a way she had come to recognize.

Jax's mum looked up from giving change to

an elderly customer. "Hi, sweetie! This is my daughter, Ellie Mae," she explained to the old lady.

"What a pretty name!" said the old lady.

"Actually, I prefer to be called Jax," said Jax for the two billionth time.

"She wants to be a scientist like her dad," Mum said. "She doesn't think 'Ellie Mae' is a suitably scientific name."

"If she's like her mother, I should think Ellie Mae can be anything she wants," the old lady told Jax's mum. "You've worked wonders with this place, dear. I don't know why, but the Dream Café always puts me in such a happy mood. I only came in for a cup of coffee, but I feel as if I've been to a really good party!"

Yup, Beans has been in, Jax thought, hiding her smile.

After the customer had finally gone on her

way, Mum tweaked Jax's souvenir cap. "So, how was the City Farm?"

"It was good!" said Jax.

"I've got something for you," her mum said. "Tell me if you think it's too gruesome to eat!" She held out a plate to Jax with a mock shudder. "Nadia's trying out some new ideas for Halloween," she explained.

Lilia's mum, Nadia, had worked at a really swanky bakery and was always inventing fun new cakes for the café. Her spooky new creation was decorated to look like a partly open coffin. A tiny jelly bat was perched on top, and sticking up out of the coffin was a severed hand.

"That is actually quite cool!" Jax said, nodding. "Nadia should put drips of red icing on the hand, though, to make it look like blood." She took a bite out of the grisly marzipan hand and laughed at her mum's queasy expression.

"Thanks for the cake, Mum! I'm going to find Beans." Still munching, she hurried out through the café and up the stairs to their flat. Jax's room was up another flight of stairs, at the top of the house. She pushed open the door and quietly peeped in.

Everything looked comfortingly the same: the space posters on her walls, her goldfish Brad busily swimming up and down his tank, her precious telescope that had belonged to her dad. Jax's dad had died in an accident when she was not quite six years old. She would never, ever stop missing him, but having his telescope helped to make him seem a little less far away.

She broke into a beaming smile as she saw

the best sight of all. Snoozing on her pillow in a patch of sunlight was a marmalade kitten.

"Wake up, lazybones!" she teased.

Moonbeans yawned as he woke and padded across the bed towards her, stretching out his furry back legs one at a time. Except for the moon sparkles glinting in his fur, Beans looked almost like a normal kitten. Of course, if he *had* been a normal kitten, Jax wouldn't have been able to hear his thoughts!

I was dreaming when you came in, he told her.

"A nice dream or a scary dream?" she asked at once.

It was a beautiful dream. I dreamed that Rumble had found my dad.

Rumble was a
battle-scarred old
tomcat with no
fixed address. He
was also one of
Beans's best friends.

"Oh, wow, Beans! Where did Rumble say
he was?"

Beans blinked at her sleepily. *You woke me up
before he could tell me.*

Jax was mortified. "Oh, Beans, I didn't know!"

Only Jax knew that Beans had a secret reason
for accepting the Aunts' mission to travel to
Planet Earth: he wanted to find his dad, whom
he had never met. All Beans knew was that his
mum had fallen in love with an Earth cat when
she was visiting our planet with a secret moon-
cat delegation. Rumble had promised to help
Moonbeans with his search and had immediately

put out the word among the other street cats. That had been months ago, but so far there had been no news.

"Would you like me to go away again?" Jax suggested humbly. "Then you might be able to get back into your dream?"

Beans gave her wrist a quick lick. *I don't need to go back to sleep. I need you to tell me about your day out at the City Farm.*

"It was fun!" she said, beaming. "I met a cat called Bandit and I think he guessed that I live with a magic moon cat, because he followed me around for practically the whole day!"

She threw herself down on her bed and, as usual, Beans took this as a hint to go trampling over her shoulder as if she was a human climbing frame, rubbing against her face as he purred. Jax closed her eyes, breathing in his other-worldly jelly-bean smell. This delicious scent was why she'd named him "Moonbeans".

What else did you see at the farm apart from Bandit? Did you see anything for me to tell the Aunts?

The Aunts were fascinated by everything to do with Planet Earth, so Jax had trained herself to look out for interesting or unusual things for Beans to tell them when he called home.

Blinking his golden eyes, Beans listened raptly as Jax told him about her day. "Which parts do you think the Aunts would like most?" she asked when she'd finished.

The giant horses, Moonbeans said at once. *And they'd be thrilled that the City Farm people are protecting rare breeds.*

Jax knew that the Aunts took an interest in *all* earthly life forms, not just human beings. "Why don't you do the Long-Distance Purr tonight and tell them?" she said at once.

The tip of Beans's tail gave the tiny twitch that meant he was amused. *You just want me to call them because you want to know if it's time for our next mission!*

By now, Jax was so used to having her mind read that she didn't even blush. "I know, because it's been *ages*. It was still summer when we helped Howard with his comedy act. It's going to be winter soon! Go on, Beans! Say you'll call them, please!" she wheedled.

The Aunts always tell us when it's the right time, Beans reminded her.

Jax puffed out her cheeks. "I know," she sighed. "Mum's always saying I have to be more patient. It's just that I really love working on missions with you, Beans." Until Moonbeans hurtled out of the sky and into her life, Jax had never seriously thought about trying to help other people. Now it was her absolutely best thing! Going on missions made her feel like a girl superhero – Ellie Mae Jackson and her magical moon cat, working to make Goose Green a better place!

Jax could only be a part-time superhero, obviously, because she had to go to school. At first she'd resented being shut up in a classroom, learning to use full stops and commas, while Beans was out exploring and making new friends. Having acquired a magical moon cat, Jax had had absolutely no intention of sharing him. But it had gradually dawned on her that Moonbeans didn't just belong to her. He was supposed to share his moon magic with everyone in Goose Green.

Jax lay softly stroking Beans, mentally running through the missions they'd completed so far. Mission Number One had been to help her mum get the Dream Café up and running. Next they'd helped Ruby-Rose, whose pushy mum had been determined to turn her into a child star, regardless of what Ruby-Rose wanted. For their last mission, Number Three, they'd helped Howard find his hidden talent. And now, of course, both Ruby-Rose and Howard were two of Jax's best friends!

With each new mission, Jax could almost feel the ripples of moon magic spreading further into the lively  streets of the city. Together, Jax and Beans were turning Goose Green into a happier, more magical place, just as the Aunts had planned.

This thought made Jax sit up with a

determined expression. "Well, I think we're going to get a new mission *really* soon. Don't twitch your tail at me, mister!" she told Moonbeans. "I'm serious – I can *feel* it in the air."

Are you sure you're not turning into a moon cat? he teased.

But Jax never got the chance to answer. Her mum was suddenly in the doorway, switching on the light and making both Jax and Moonbeans blink at her like owls.

"Have you closed the café already?" Jax said in surprise. Deep in conversation with Beans, she hadn't even noticed it getting dark.

"I've closed the café and now I fancy sausage

and mash – how about you?" said Mum with a smile.

"Sausage and mash with your special onion gravy?" said Jax at once.

Mum laughed. "Special onion gravy it is!"

Jax was still spooning up the last tasty drops of gravy when the phone rang. It was Ruby-Rose. She sounded upset.

"What's wrong?" Jax asked.

"It's Conrad," Ruby-Rose gulped. "I walked back home with him and his little brothers. He still seemed really down, so I said he'd better cheer up soon because it's nearly his birthday. I was only teasing, Jax, but he almost bit my head off. He said he didn't need spoiled little stage-school brats like me telling him what to do." Jax could hear her sniffing back tears. "I was just trying to be his friend, Jax," she sobbed.

"Conrad knows that really," Jax told her quickly.

"And I'm not a stage-school brat," Ruby-Rose wailed. "Not any more, I'm not."

"He knows that too," Jax said soothingly. "He probably just got super-tired walking around the farm and wanted to take it out on somebody."

"He did say he was so excited the night before that he couldn't sleep," Ruby-Rose remembered.

"There you go," Jax said in the same soothing voice. "I bet tomorrow he'll be his normal nutty self again."

"Thanks, Jax!" Ruby-Rose sounded a bit less tearful now.

They talked for a little longer, then Jax said goodbye to her friend and went back to eat her pudding, a cherry-flavoured yoghurt.

Mum looked concerned. "Is Ruby-Rose okay?"

Jax shook her head. "She's worried about Conrad."

Mum frowned. "Didn't you have problems with Conrad when you first started at Goose Green Primary School? Wasn't he bullying Lilia?"

"That was ages ago," Jax said fiercely. "Conrad isn't like that now. He's good mates with nearly everyone and he tries really hard in lessons. Everyone says he's totally changed."

"Oh well, perhaps he was just having a bad day," said Mum.

"Maybe," said Jax, doubtfully.

Upstairs, Jax wandered over to her window and looked out at the trees blowing in the wind. Beans was out there somewhere – he'd gone out for one of his walks just before she went downstairs to have her tea. *Beans always liked Conrad*, she comforted herself. The magical moon cat had seen through Conrad the bully to the real Conrad underneath straight away…

When Jax had first started at Goose Green Primary School, Conrad was always picking on other children, and threatening to karate-kick them. But Jax had quickly realized that Conrad didn't have a clue how to do karate! Jax *did* know how to do karate – and though her karate teacher had made his students promise they would never use it to hurt anyone, he'd never said they couldn't use it to give someone a bit of a shock.

So, one day, Jax had smuggled an invisible Moonbeans into school. And when Conrad had started tormenting Lilia during their lunch break, Jax and Beans decided to teach him a lesson he wouldn't forget. Launching herself at an astonished Conrad, Jax had done her best flying karate-kick.

As she flew through the air, brightly-coloured stars had come fizzing and flashing from her hands and feet! Of course, Conrad hadn't known that a magical moon cat was behind these astonishing firework effects, and he'd been so shocked that he'd completely stopped his bullying ways. Gradually, he and Jax had become good friends.

Jax could only think that the school trip had unsettled Conrad in some way. She just didn't understand why. Despite what Howard said, she couldn't see why the happiest day of someone's life would make them turn mean.

Downstairs, the cat flap give a sharp *thwack!*

Beans was back. She heard his paws thundering upstairs as if he was being pursued by runaway horses. He burst into her room, wild-eyed.

"Beans, what's wrong?" She crouched to give him a soothing stroke, but he nimbly skipped away, too excited to be touched.

I've just seen Rumble, he told her. *He thinks he's found my dad!*

His name is Mungo

3

Jax was still sitting on the floor open-mouthed, with a million questions fighting to get out, when her mum walked in. She parked herself down on the bed, obviously in the mood for a chat. "Your grandpa just phoned," she said, beaming. "He's coming over on Saturday to fix the bathroom tap and he says he's bringing you a special present!"

"That's great," Jax said politely. Normally she'd be happy to chat about her grandpa, whom she loved dearly – not to mention the possibility of a present. But just at this moment, she *really* wished her mum would go away! Moonbeans was carefully washing as if nothing had happened, but Jax could feel him secretly fizzing with excitement.

"He's totally changed his attitude since you invited him to the school talent show," her mum went on. "You know what, Ellie Mae? After we moved to Goose Green, I think your silly grandpa actually convinced himself we didn't need him. That's the reason he was acting so grumpy!"

"Yes, I know," Jax said without thinking. All her attention was on a trembling, excited Moonbeans. If he had to wait any longer to tell her his news, she thought he'd go fizzing off into space like a Roman candle.

"How did you know?" her mum asked, surprised.

Moonbeans told me. "Oh, I don't know," she said vaguely. "I just kind of figured it out." In her desperation, Jax faked a yawn. "Sorry, Mum, I'm really tired."

"Of course you are, sweetie." Her mum looked guilty. "I forgot you've had such a long day. Do you want a hot-water bottle? It's turned so chilly tonight. It feels almost like winter!"

"It's okay, I've already got one!" Jax pointed at Beans with a grin.

Her mum laughed. Kissing Jax goodnight, she hurried back downstairs.

Jax jumped into her PJs and switched off her bedside lamp. She was too excited to get under the covers, so she just perched on the edge of her bed. She could feel her heart beating super-fast. "We can talk now," she whispered.

Beans jumped up beside her, his golden eyes glowing in the dark.

"So where *is* he?" she asked softly. "Where's your dad?"

I don't know where he is but I know who he's with, Beans said.

Jax was baffled. "But if you know who he's with surely you can figure out *where* he is?"

Not if they're travelling around the country, Beans said enigmatically.

Jax was totally confused now. "I don't get it."

He's with a travelling circus! Beans explained.

She gasped. "Beans, that's SO cool! How did Rumble find out?"

He heard it from a street cat called Gizmo, who heard it from Claws, who heard it from Lefty, who heard it from Fish Face…
Beans went on reeling off names. Jax assumed they were the names of street cats, but they sounded

more like gangsters! …*who heard it from
Thin Lizzie, who heard it from Gnasher,
who heard it from Sammy the
Spider, who heard it from
Bandit at the City Farm,*
Beans finished at last.

Laughing out loud at
"Sammy the Spider", Jax
almost missed what he'd said,
but then her eyes went wide. "Bandit seriously
knows your dad?"

*Bandit doesn't know my dad, but he's made
friends with a pony who used to perform with
his circus.*

Jax gave a little gasp. "Not Spangle?"

Beans was surprised. *Yes, how did you know?*

"I saw her this afternoon! We saw so many
animals that I forgot to tell you. So what did
Spangle say about your dad?"

Beans delicately washed a paw. *She said he's extremely handsome, totally black like a panther, apart from a single white whisker, and he's got unusually large golden eyes.*

"Just like yours," Jax breathed.

Are my eyes unusually large? Moonbeans asked, surprised.

"Beans, they're like headlamps! So did Rumble tell you your dad's name?"

It's Mungo, said Moonbeans proudly. *Do you think that's a good name for a cat?*

"I think it's a *great* name," she told him warmly. "Do you know which circus he's with?"

Rumble didn't know. Beans looked dejected for a moment, then perked up again. *We could go to the City Farm this weekend and find out!*

"Good idea!" Jax wasn't quite sure how

they'd get there, but she didn't want to ruin her little moon cat's big moment by worrying about tiny details. "Wow, Beans! You're going to meet your dad really soon! Aren't you excited?"

Excited and scared, he confessed. *I've wished for this for so long. Now it's happening, it feels strange, almost like a dream.*

"Does your dad actually perform in the circus?"

I don't think Rumble knows. Beans looked downcast again.

"Never mind, you can ask Spangle on Saturday," Jax said quickly. A big yawn took her by surprise. Her mum was right. It had been a long day. "Sorry, Beans. I'm getting a bit sleepy," she confessed.

Beans came to curl up on her pillow as he did every night. Usually they chatted together in the dark until one or both of them fell asleep. But tonight Beans immediately jumped up again. *I can't sleep. My paws feel too fizzy!*

Jax often felt too fizzy to sleep, so she sympathized. "My dad sometimes sang to me when I couldn't sleep," she told him. "I'll sing his song to you if you like?"

I'd like that, Beans said gratefully.

Jax had to clear her throat a few times before she shyly started singing her dad's song about a lonely yellow bird high in a banana tree.

The last time Dad had sung it to her, Jax wasn't quite six years old. She was nine and a half now, but she still remembered every word. She was careful to sing it just the same way her dad used to, very softly and slowly, to make it like a proper lullaby, and as she sang, she felt Beans gradually relax. In no time, he was asleep, just occasionally letting out a squeaky little purr.

Jax lay staring wistfully up at her glow-stars. Singing his special lullaby had brought back other memories of her dad; like the smell of his shaving soap, and that little sparkle in his eyes when Jax or Mum made him laugh. She would do anything to have him back again. *Poor Beans has never even set eyes on his dad*, she thought. *No wonder he's so desperate to find him.*

Jax had a sudden alarming thought. Suppose, when Beans had found his dad, he no longer needed Jax? *That's just silly*, she told herself fiercely. *Beans and I are going to be together for ever and ever.*

And she drifted into a dream where she and Moonbeans were at the circus. Clowns, jugglers and acrobats performed breathtaking stunts, watched by a big black cat with a single gleaming white whisker and enormous golden eyes.

Next morning, Mum's alarm clock failed to go off and Jax and her mum went rushing around in a panic. Mum was yelling things like, "Where's my  hairbrush? I can't open the café looking like a mophead!" while Jax was wailing, "Mum, I can't find my gym things!"

Jax *hated* these kinds of mornings! She set off to meet Lilia with the worrying feeling that she'd forgotten something crucial. She sometimes had a dream where she turned up at school in her underwear, and she always worried it would eventually happen for real.

The first person she and Lilia saw when they walked through the school gates was Conrad, moodily kicking a ball. Normally he'd have rushed straight over to them, cracking jokes at a mile a minute. This morning, he just turned his back and deliberately took his ball off to a different part of the playground.

Lilia and Jax looked at each other.

"He is SO not in a good mood," Lilia said in a low voice. "What do you think is the matter?"

Jax shook her head. "I'm not sure." She only knew that she missed the cheerful cheeky Conrad and wished she could bring him back.

"We could try to cheer him up," Lilia suggested.

"Ruby-Rose tried that last night," Jax told her friend. "She said he almost bit her head off."

"We should still try," Lilia said firmly.

They made their way over to Conrad.

"Look, tell us if you'd rather be alone—" Jax started.

"I would, actually, so push off," Conrad said rudely.

Jax didn't think this was a very hopeful start, but she made herself carry on. "It's just…if something's wrong, you know—"

"So what if there is?" he glowered.

"We're your friends," Jax said bravely. "Friends are supposed to help each other."

Conrad didn't seem to want to meet her eyes. "You can't," he growled. "No one can."

"We might be able to," Lilia said, swallowing, "if you told us what was wrong."

"Look, leave me alone, will you?" Conrad burst out. "If you want to know, I asked my parents if I could have a puppy last night. They said no way!"

"Puppies *are* a lot of work," said Lilia in her gentlest voice.

"You could ask them if they'll let you have a kitten or a rabbit instead?" Jax suggested.

"Don't you think I already tried that?" he said angrily. "They said I can't have a puppy. I can't have a kitten or a rabbit or a guinea pig. I can't have a pet full stop, because my little brother is allergic! Are you happy now?" Conrad folded his arms and stood glowering at Jax.

But before she could answer, the bell went for the start of school and everybody had to line up to go inside.

The first lesson was English, but Jax couldn't concentrate. Their conversation with Conrad had left her feeling hurt and also angry. Conrad wasn't being fair. He seemed really mad with her about something, but she didn't think she'd done anything wrong. Now and then she cautiously glanced across at him, but he was always stonily looking the other way. She caught Ruby-Rose sneaking looks at him too.

Jax decided she'd have it out with him at break. She was really sorry that Conrad's parents wouldn't allow him to keep a pet, but he had no right to take it out on his friends! When the bell rang, she marched out into the playground, determined to give him a piece of her mind.

To her amazement, Conrad was happily charging around with some other boys. He looked almost exactly like the friendly pre-City Farm Conrad.

Lilia and Ruby-Rose caught up with her as she watched him, bewildered.

He gave them a cheerful wave. "Hello, girls!"

Ruby-Rose beamed at Jax. "Jax, you were right! Conrad must have just been tired. He's totally fine now!"

Jax frowned. Conrad hadn't been quite so fine an hour or so ago. She wondered what had happened to cheer him up.

Whatever it was, it put Conrad in a good mood for the rest of the day. During art, Jax actually heard him singing under his breath.

At home time, she and Lilia grabbed their coats and hurried out into the windy playground. They had just reached the gate when a gust of wind snatched Jax's scarf and she had to dash back to rescue it.

To her surprise, Conrad was still in the playground, chatting to a boy from the class above theirs. She bent down to pick up her scarf and as she straightened up, she saw the boys shaking hands; almost as if they were making some kind of deal.

Quickly retying her scarf, Jax ran to catch up with Lilia. She couldn't wait to be home in the warm with Moonbeans. They had secret plans to make if they were going to find the mysterious Mungo.

"You look like a girl in need of hot chocolate," Mum said when Jax walked in.

"I'm in need of hot chocolate with extra marshmallows," Jax told her. "My face is really cold from the wind – feel!"

Jax waited till her mum had finished frothing up the milk, then, remembering her promise to Moonbeans, she took a deep breath and asked if Mum would take her to the City Farm on Saturday.

Mum looked astonished. "But you just went!"

"I know, but it was so good I want to go again with you! You'd love it, Mum, I know you would," she wheedled.

"I don't think I would, sweetie. Fur and feathers, remember?"

Jax felt her heart drop into her shoes. She had temporarily forgotten that her mum was allergic to practically everything in the universe. Beans was the only cat Mum had ever met who didn't make her sneeze, probably because he came from a totally different world.

Jax had been lucky. The Aunts had sent her

61

Moonbeans. It suddenly occurred to Jax that her wish for a cute kitten had come true, while Conrad, who loved animals every bit as much as Jax, wasn't even allowed to have a tiny little gerbil. *Life is so unfair sometimes*, she thought, and suddenly she didn't feel nearly so mad with Conrad.

Mum was dropping tiny pastel-coloured marshmallows into Jax's hot chocolate, before she finally handed her the mug. She gave Jax an apologetic smile. "Even if I wasn't allergic, sweetie, I couldn't leave the café. Saturdays are our busiest time. One day, when I can afford to pay more staff, we'll have days out together, but not just yet. I'm sorry."

Jax swallowed. "It's not your fault."

She went upstairs to break the bad news to Beans. "Beans, I'm so sorry," she wailed. "I feel like I've really let you down."

To her surprise, Moonbeans didn't seem too worried. *You'll find a way.* He looked so trusting that Jax could have cried. She couldn't bear it – she'd *have* to get him to the City Farm somehow.

She sat down at her desk to do her homework and Beans settled by her elbow. When he tucked his paws underneath like that, Jax thought he looked exactly like a fluffy mother hen. She could see he was miles away, gazing dreamily into space. *He's thinking about his dad*, she thought. At least Jax could remember what it was like to have a loving dad – Beans had never had that. No wonder he couldn't think about anything else.

How am I going to get him to the farm, though? she worried. She knew her mum would never let her go all that way by herself.

As if the Aunts had breathed it into her ear,

Jax had a sudden brainwave. *Grandpa!* Mum had said he was coming over on Saturday! *I'll ask him to take me to the farm*, she thought. *I'll phone him after school tomorrow.*

Relieved to have a plan at last, Jax finally managed to concentrate on her homework.

Later, after Jax was tucked up in bed and her mum had been in to say goodnight, Jax asked Beans, "Have you heard from the Aunts yet about our new mission?"

Not yet, he said.

Jax had known, really, that he hadn't. It was her way of reminding him that they were still supposed to be a team: Ellie Mae Jackson and her magical moon cat. Because, right at this moment, Jax wasn't sure if he *did* remember.

Moonbeans was curled up beside her, but his thoughts still seemed far away. *Tell me about*

circuses, he said suddenly. *I don't know what they're like.*

Jax told him about a circus she'd been to with her mum and dad when she was little. She put in all the details she could remember: the circus ring full of fresh sawdust, clowns with huge painted-on smiles and even huger shoes, acrobats in leotards, the ringmaster in his shiny black top hat. Moonbeans listened, wide-eyed, as if Jax was telling him a magical bedtime story.

After she'd finished telling him about the circus, Beans still felt too fizzy to sleep, so Jax sang "Yellow Bird" again. Soon he was snoring cute little moon-kitten snores.

Jax stared up at her glow-stars, feeling soft
kitten fur tickling her cheek and breathing in
a magical smell of jelly beans. Inside her chest,
her heart felt unusually heavy, as if it was
slowly turning into stone.

She knew that if someone was to tell her
that her dad was still alive on a far-distant
world, she'd have to rush
to find him too. The
problem was, once
she'd found him, she
seriously doubted if
she'd ever be able to let

him go. Suppose Beans found his dad and
decided to stay with him for ever? Jax would be
all alone again. The idea that she might lose
Beans made Jax feel as if she couldn't breathe.

A tiny voice in her head whispered, *If Beans*

goes off with his dad, I'll be just like Conrad.
A tear tried to crawl down the side of her nose, but Jax fiercely swiped it away. *This isn't about you, Ellie Mae Jackson,* she scolded. *This is about a little moon cat that you happen to love very much.*

No matter how unhappy it made her, Jax was determined to do the right thing. It was all very well, the Aunts sending Beans to Goose Green to help everyone live happier lives, but she thought Beans deserved to be happy too.

Major big trouble

4

"Conrad's acting really weird today, isn't he?" Lilia whispered at school the next day, halfway through their first lesson.

Jax nodded. It was true. Conrad had kept his huge parka on all through assembly then kicked up a big fuss at the start of lessons when Mrs. Chaudhary told him he had to take it off. He'd stormed off to hang it up in the school cloakrooms with the other children's coats, and when he returned to the classroom he had pulled his shirt collar up to his chin and his sweater sleeves down as far as his thumbs!

Even his expression was weird, Jax thought. He looked guilty and kind of jumpy.

Now everyone was supposed to be writing about what they hoped to be doing in ten years' time. Jax had decided to write about having an exciting life as a world-famous space scientist. She got so carried away that she actually  snapped her pencil! On her way to use the class pencil sharpener, she passed Conrad's table and saw that he'd scrawled: *In ten years' time, I will be a person who—*

But Jax wasn't able to read what Conrad was going to be, because he'd angrily crossed the next few words out several times. As she watched, he grabbed at one of his cuffs, yanking it down over his hand. Then he pulled his collar up almost to his ears.

At break time, Conrad put his parka back on and went out into the playground with his furry hood pulled up as if he was expecting blizzards. One of Conrad's mates called him to join in a kick-about in the playground and he just shook his head.

It was the same at lunchtime; Conrad wearing his big parka zipped up to his chin, avoiding his friends, with the same weirdly jumpy expression on his face.

Jax thought she'd go to find Howard in case he knew what was wrong with Conrad. The boys had been friends since Conrad had introduced Howard's stand-up routine in the school talent show.

She eventually tracked him down in the school library.

"Has Conrad said anything to you?" she asked.

"Like what?" Howard closed the book he'd been reading.

"Like, if something's really wrong. You've got to admit, he's being seriously strange."

"He's a bit on edge," Howard admitted. "And he *really* doesn't want to take that coat off!"

Jax sighed. It seemed that Howard was every bit as puzzled as she was. She wished Moonbeans was there to tell them what Conrad was thinking.

That afternoon, Conrad was still acting weird. Once he let out a surprised giggle, clutching at his sweater.

Suddenly Lilia gasped. "What's that funny lump on Conrad's back?"

Jax gasped too. The lump was on the move, becoming a speedy bulge that rapidly disappeared over his shoulder. She spotted another smaller lump travelling up the inside of his sleeve. The lumps were *alive*!

The next minute, a small whiskery nose popped out of the back of his collar.

Conrad reached around to make a grab for it, and the nose disappeared back inside his shirt. Then he made another grab at the cuff of his sweater. Something dropped on to the floor – *plop* – and went speeding under the tables like a tiny clockwork car.

Jasmine screamed. "*Miss*, there's a *rat*!"

The rest of the class jumped out of their seats in a panic. Mrs. Chaudhary clapped her hands to restore order. "Okay, everyone, try to stay calm. I want you all to line up and leave the classroom quickly and quietly."

"No, *don't*!" Conrad was frantic. "Please, Miss, everybody's got to stay exactly where they are or someone might tread on him!"

Mrs. Chaudhary just ignored him. "Howard,

I want you to go down to the headmaster's office. Tell him I'm taking everybody into the hall and ask him to contact the pest control people immediately."

"*Miss!*" Jax was desperately waving her arm. "It's not a rat. I *saw* it! It's just a little baby mouse. Tell her, Conrad," she whispered. "She's going to find out in the end."

Jax saw Conrad's freckled face slowly turning red.

Mrs. Chaudhary folded her arms. "Is there something you'd like to tell me, Conrad?"

Jax heard him swallow. "It's just a baby mouse, Miss, like Jax said. I've got his little brother up my sleeve, look!"  He rolled up the cuff of his sweater and gently removed the mouse from its hiding place.

73

Meanwhile, Jax and Howard were silently stalking the other mouse.

At last it scuttled into a corner by the art cupboard and curled up into a furry little ball, seeming to think it was now invisible.

Jax tiptoed closer and closer to the mouse. "*Got* it!" she said softly, gently scooping it up.

Everybody crowded round her to see.

"Aw, it's *sooo* cute!" said Bella.

Jax could feel the mouse's tiny heart beating rapidly against her palm. "We're going to need a box," she told Howard.

She stroked the snow-white mouse with the tip of her finger. It looked exactly like a sugar mouse, except for its quivering little whiskers.

Howard was rummaging through the art cupboard, where he found a shoebox and some shredded paper, which he put into the bottom of the box. He borrowed a biro and used it to pierce several holes in the box lid. "We'll put sticky tape on to stop them escaping," he told Conrad with a smile.

"They won't be in there long," Jax said, trying to comfort him. "It's just until you get them back home."

Conrad just looked as if he wished the ground would swallow him up, and didn't say a word.

"Poor Conrad," Lilia said softly. "He's in major big trouble."

At home time, Jax saw Conrad and his mum and Conrad's little brothers walking out through the school gates. Jax could hear her scolding: "I trusted you, Conrad. I thought you'd turned over a new leaf. I need you to be the responsible one now Lenny's left home. You're supposed to set an example to your little brothers."

Conrad was a picture of misery as his mum continued to tell him off. There was no sign of the shoebox, Jax realized with a pang. On top of everything else, his mum hadn't even let him keep the mice.

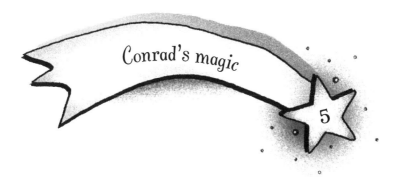

Conrad's magic

5

At home, Jax poured out the story of Conrad and the mice to her mum. Luckily the café was really quiet, so Mum had time to listen. Jax was surprised to see that she didn't seem to be that shocked. In fact, Jax thought Mum might actually be trying not to laugh.

"Your grandpa was always getting into trouble for taking animals and insects into school when he was a boy," Mum said. "Once a frog escaped from his pocket and jumped into the teacher's handbag! He got into big trouble for that!"

Jax giggled, amazed. "Seriously? Grandpa actually took a frog to school!" She tried to imagine him as a mischievous little boy, keeping frogs in his pocket.

"Would it help to cheer Conrad up if you took him a really spooky cake tomorrow?" her mum asked.

Jax nodded eagerly. "Definitely!"

"Pick one you think he'd like," her mum said, "and I'll put it in one of our special Halloween cake boxes."

There were certainly plenty to choose from. Nadia had been super-busy, and Mum's cake display cabinet was filled with spectacularly  gruesome cakes. There were miniature pumpkins with ghoulish grins, cupcakes dripping with pretend slime and decorated with sugar

spiderwebs and jelly bats, cakes
with spooky skulls made from
white chocolate…one
cupcake just said *BOO!*

Jax picked out the spookiest
cake in the cabinet for her friend. Talking
about Grandpa had reminded her of her plan
to get him to take her and Beans to the City
Farm at the weekend. "Mum, since you can't
take me to the City Farm on Saturday, would
it be okay if Grandpa took me instead?" she
asked.

"That's a brilliant idea!" said her mum. "I
don't know why I didn't think of it myself! Why
don't you call him now and ask him?"

Grandpa picked up the phone straight away.
He sounded pleased to hear her voice. "Hello,
Ellie Mae, what are you up to these days?"

"Forget about *me*! Mum's just been telling

me all the things *you* got up to when you were my age," Jax teased.

He laughed. "Your mother doesn't know the half of it!"

Beans had suddenly appeared in the sitting room doorway, washing the tip of his tail with great care. Jax could tell he was listening in to her call.

"Grandpa, I actually phoned for a favour."

"Don't say you need me to do my famous grandpa chuckle at another talent show?" he joked at once.

"Not this time, Grandpa!" Crossing her fingers for luck, Jax said, "Our class went to the City Farm this week, and I loved it so much that I really want to go again. Mum thought you'd love it too. Could you maybe take me this weekend? They've got shire horses!" she added breathlessly.

She heard Beans start his special Purr of Power, but as it turned out, her grandpa didn't need any persuading. "I'd be delighted," he said warmly. "Shire horses, you say?"

Jax grinned at Beans and stuck up her thumb.

He said yes, didn't he? Beans said excitedly when she got off the phone. *That means I'll really get to talk to Spangle.* He stood perfectly still for a moment, then his eyes went huge and wild and he started madly chasing his tail to let out some of his excitement.

Since Jax didn't have a tail to chase she just said, "*Woo-hoo*, Beans! We DID it!" Then she picked him up and hugged him until he squeaked.

That night Jax didn't need to sing "Yellow Bird". Moonbeans fell asleep straight away. It was Jax who lay awake, listening to the church clock strike midnight as her brain jumped between worrying about Conrad, to panicking about losing Beans.

Suddenly she saw two amber-gold eyes staring at her accusingly. *Why are you still awake?*

"I'm not sure," she fibbed. "Maybe it's because it's nearly Halloween."

What's Halloween? he asked.

"It's supposed to be the one day in the year when all kinds of spooky and magical creatures are able to get into our world and cause mischief," Jax explained.

It sounds a bit scary, Beans said nervously.

"It's a *bit* scary," she agreed, "but mostly it's good fun. Children dress up in weird costumes and go round the streets trick-or-treating! You knock on people's doors and if they don't give you a treat you can play a funny trick – but they almost always give you a treat!"

Can I go trick-or-treating with you? Beans said at once.

"You *totally* can!" Jax promised, though that little whispering voice in her head added forlornly: *If you're still here.*

If Halloween is so much fun, why does it stop you going to sleep? Beans asked, puzzled.

Jax sat up with a sigh. "It doesn't really. I just said that, Beans. I'm actually *really* worried about Conrad."

Why? What's the matter with him? Beans said anxiously.

Jax quickly explained about Conrad and the mice. "He's really good with animals, Beans. I mean, REALLY good. You should have seen him at the City Farm. But his little brother's got allergies, so he's not allowed to have even one tiny little pet."

Why didn't you tell me all this before? Beans demanded.

"Because…well, you had a lot on your mind with finding your dad and everything." Jax was trying to be tactful.

For a moment Beans avoided her eyes. *I've just been thinking about myself, haven't I?* he said humbly.

Jax was mortified. "I never said that!"

But it's true! Conrad's in trouble and you didn't feel you could tell me.

"Well, I'm telling you now," she said gently. "Can you think of a way to help him? He's so desperate for a pet of his own, but there just doesn't seem like any way he can have one."

What Conrad needs, Beans said, *is more magic in his life.*

Jax stared at him. She hadn't expected him to say that.

That day in the playground, when I made stars come out of your hands and feet – that's when he started to change.  Beans was absolutely certain.

Jax felt tears prickle behind her eyelids. For the first time she understood that Conrad hadn't just stopped bullying because Beans and Jax had given him a big fright. He'd stopped because he'd had a glimpse of *magic*. That one tiny glimpse had shown Conrad that the world was far more wonderful than he'd thought, and he'd totally turned over a new leaf.

But things had gone downhill for Conrad since then. His big brother, Lenny, had left home. With Lenny gone, their hard-working mum and dad needed Conrad to help out, doing Lenny's chores and looking after his three little brothers. Though he was still just a kid himself, he no longer had time to do anything nutty and fun. That magical moment in the playground must have seemed like a far-away dream.

Then, at the City Farm, Conrad had found magic of a different kind; his *own* special magic. Jax suddenly remembered him surrounded by playful puppies, his face one big grin. But for some reason, finding his special magic had made Conrad feel worse, not better. He had discovered what he *needed* to be happy – lots and lots of animals! – but he couldn't seem to figure out what he had to do to *get* it.

He needs a moon cat, Jax thought, cuddling up to a purring Moonbeans. That was the one really unfair difference between her and Conrad. For six whole months, Jax had had a magical moon cat to share her troubles and have adventures with. Even supposing that Moonbeans couldn't stay for ever (and she really, *really* hoped he could), Jax would always know that magical moon cats existed. She would always know that the universe was a wonderful and magical place. She wished she could tell Conrad that.

I hope we get to go on at least one more mission, she thought, snuggling closer to her little moon cat. In the meantime, she was determined to cheer up Conrad. Breathing in the other-worldly smell of jelly beans, Jax fell asleep at last.

The Big School Clean-up

Next morning, it seemed like everyone in their school had heard the story of Conrad and the mice. In assembly, children pointed and sniggered.

Conrad tried to act as if he hadn't noticed, but he'd gone as red as a postbox. He stared miserably at the floor as Mr. Tattersall complained about the litter that kept blowing into the playground.

"I want people in Goose Green to see that our pupils take real pride in their school," he told them. "So from today, at lunchtime, the children in the top two classes are going to help clear up. Your teachers will provide all the necessary equipment."

"That's us, Jax," Lilia whispered behind her hand.

Conrad didn't even seem to be listening.

In class he went to sit at a table by himself. When Jax and her friends tried to talk to him, he ignored them. Jax wasn't worried, though, not yet, because she had something that she thought would help to cure Conrad's bad mood.

At break time, she made her way across the playground to where Conrad stood hunched miserably inside his coat. "I've brought you something," she told him, whipping the lid off the small decorated cake box. "Ta-da!"

Conrad was always hungry and he especially loved sweet things. Plus, like all boys, he had a bizarre sense of humour! Jax was sure he couldn't resist the cupcake she'd picked out for him. Dripping green sugar "slime", it was topped with a bandaged mummy made out of white chocolate, a dark chocolate beetle, and a jelly rat.

She was wrong.

"I don't want your stupid cake," he told her scornfully, and walked off without another word.

Jax was officially worried now. Conrad was really mad, she could feel it, but she just didn't know what to do. If Beans was right, Conrad was mad because he'd had a glimpse of magic and it had been taken away. The City Farm had shown him what he *really* loved – being with animals – but he couldn't have it. She knew she had to do something to help him – but what?

For the rest of the morning, Jax didn't hear a word her teacher said – she was so worried.

After lunch, it was time for Mr. Tattersall's Big School Clean-up. Mrs. Chaudhary issued everyone with rubber gloves and a special pointed stick for picking up litter.

Conrad trudged into the playground with the others and started drearily picking up fast-food wrappers. Jax followed. She longed to talk to him, but she couldn't think what to say. She wanted to give Conrad a tiny bit of hope that his life could get better, but she didn't know how.

For a few minutes they filled their rubbish bags in silence. It wasn't a comfortable silence and Conrad's expression was the opposite of friendly.

Quite suddenly, Jax decided it was now or never. With no time to plan what to say, she blurted out, "Do you believe in magic?"

Conrad stabbed at a piece of litter and dropped it in his sack. "Do you think I'm stupid or something?" he snarled.

Jax swallowed. "I don't think you're stupid. It's just that I do – believe in magic, I mean."

"Yeah, well you're a girl. Girls love believing in fairies and all that rubbish," Conrad said scornfully.

Jax wasn't standing for that! "I don't know about fairies but I do know about karate!" she blazed. "Or have you forgotten what happened that time?"

Conrad's expression didn't change but he went very still. *Oops*, Jax thought. The words had just slipped out. She was almost sure that he was picturing a girl with brilliant coloured stars flashing from her hands and feet.

"I thought I dreamed that," he said almost to himself.

"No," she whispered. "It was real."

Neither of them spoke for a moment but Jax saw something change in Conrad's eyes.

"I knew I couldn't have a dog. I knew that," he told her huskily. "My baby brother's allergic. My dad's away all the time and my mum's busy with work and my brothers. But then I thought, *Well, why not get a little mouse?*"

"You got *two* mice," Jax pointed out.

"Because I thought one would get lonely," he explained gruffly.

"Yes but, Conrad, bringing them to school was *asking* for trouble."

"I know that *now*! I never thought it through, did I?" Conrad sounded angry with himself. "I just thought I'd keep them in a little box in my room. I was like, *Who's to know?* But then Mum said she'd got a few days

93

off and she was going to clean our rooms!
I couldn't let her find them, could I?"

Jax shook her head. "I suppose not."

"I just brought two little mice into school,
that's all," Conrad said bitterly, "but my mum
gets called down to the headmaster and it's all
'Conrad this', 'Conrad that', just like the old
days."

Jax gently touched his sleeve. "Conrad,
suppose somebody could make your dream
come true. Would you let them do it?"

Conrad speared a sweet wrapper with his
stick. Instead of dropping it in the sack, he
turned to Jax. For a moment she saw real
longing in his face.

"Conrad! Ellie Mae!" a teacher yelled.
"You're supposed to be keeping your school
tidy, not having a private chat!"

Conrad scowled. "I hate being a kid," he

muttered under his breath. "Everyone's always telling us what to do. Nobody cares what *we* want."

Still scowling, he went back to picking up litter.

By home time, Jax was desperate to tell Beans all about her conversation with Conrad.

In the café, the air was only very faintly pink and shimmery, suggesting that it had been a while since Moonbeans had stopped by to charm her mum's customers.

Jax raced upstairs, expecting to find the little moon cat curled up on her bed, but her room was empty. *That's weird*, she thought. Beans usually made a point of being home when Jax got back from school.

Suddenly she thought, *I bet he's in the garden*, and went rushing back downstairs.

But when she reached the back door, for no reason that she could explain, she suddenly stopped. Then, very softly turning the handle, she cautiously peeped out into the autumn dusk – and gasped.

Just as she'd thought, Moonbeans *was* in the garden – but he wasn't alone. He was deep in conversation with local "life forms", as he called them.

There were four or five rascally-looking street cats, all carefully ignoring each other. Cautiously keeping out of the way of the cats  were three enormous pigeons and one small fluffy baby pigeon. As if this wasn't strange enough, there was an entire family of urban foxes – a mother, a father and two playful little cubs – plus something that Jax at first took to

be a rather peculiar
supersized scrubbing
brush until she realized
she was looking at a
real live hedgehog.

She watched for a moment, transfixed,
afraid to breathe or move, then she silently
closed the door. She couldn't imagine why this
mysterious meeting had been called, but she
had a feeling it was important, and she didn't
want to scare the creatures away.

Darkness fell and still Moonbeans didn't
come indoors. Mum closed the café for the day,
and then she and Jax ate their supper in the
kitchen.

After they'd washed up, Jax went up to her
room and tried to concentrate on her
homework. Now and then she'd run to the
window, peering out into the darkness,

wondering if the strange meeting was still going on.

Jax was in bed, half asleep, by the time Moonbeans eventually came indoors. He deliberately nudged her with his cold nose to wake her, making her sit up with a gasp. His fur smelled of jelly beans mixed with night and frost and just a hint of autumn bonfires.

Jax rubbed her eyes. "What's going on, Beans?"

I've been talking to some local life forms, he said calmly.

"I know, I saw you! But you've been ages! You haven't seriously been talking all this time?"

Yes, because some life forms only come out at night, he explained.

"You mean like rats and beetles?" Jax said nervously.

And moths, Beans said. *Humans always forget about moths, I don't know why.*

"But what did they all *want*?" Jax asked, bewildered.

Beans didn't answer. *Did you see that baby pigeon?* he asked.

Jax nodded, too confused to speak.

A few days ago, it got its foot trapped in a soft-drink can. Conrad freed it. They told me lots of stories like that.

"Lots of stories like what?" Jax was still feeling muddled.

Stories about Conrad, helping birds and animals. Did you know he went round to all the neighbours and asked them to rake up their dead leaves really carefully. He said sometimes sleepy hibernating hedgehogs accidentally ended up on

bonfires on November 5th, and he didn't want that to happen.

"Conrad did that?" said Jax, amazed.

Beans blinked his golden eyes. *You were right*, he said. *Conrad really cares about animals.*

Jax nodded, remembering Conrad pleading with everyone to keep still so they wouldn't hurt the mouse. "But why would they come to see you about Conrad, though? It seems, you know, a bit random."

It wasn't random at all. Beans seemed slightly huffy. *They'd heard about our mission. They know we're trying to make Goose Green a happier place, and they wondered if we'd help Conrad.*

Jax suddenly grasped what Beans was telling her. "You mean they came to ask if he could be our next mission?" she breathed.

Yes! Beans blinked his amber-gold eyes,

relieved that she finally understood. *I knew that would make you happy*, he said, giving his paw a brief wash. *It does make you happy, doesn't it?* he inquired anxiously.

"It makes me *really* happy!" she reassured him, beaming.

She gave a gasp as the first bright pink sparkles came softly floating down through the dark. The Aunts were letting them know that they were in total agreement with the life forms of Goose Green. The kindly extraterrestrials only sent sparkles when it was time for a new mission. It seemed like everyone, not just Jax, thought it was time that Conrad had a helping hand.

With the pink sparkles gently raining all around, Jax couldn't stop smiling. It was official! Conrad was their next mission!

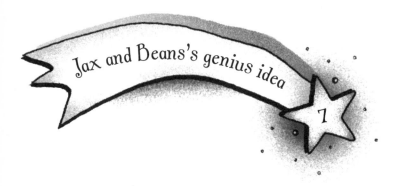

"Shall I put the hook here or here, Ellie?" Grandpa called from the stepladder.

"The first place you tried," Jax told him. "I can't believe you got me an actual mobile of the solar system! I totally love it, Grandpa." What with their new mission and Beans's search for his father, Jax had completely forgotten that her grandpa had promised to bring her a present!

"Well, I know you're into all this space malarkey." Grandpa screwed in the cup hook, then carefully looped the mobile over it.

"Does that look all right to you?"

Jax just nodded, lost for words. Grandpa's mobile looked much better than all right. The sun, the moon and all the planets were there in their 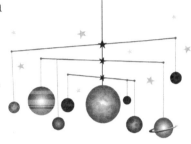 proper orbits: Mars and Neptune, Jupiter and Saturn, Uranus, Venus, tiny Mercury – and Earth, the beautiful blue-green planet that was her home. It was like having a tiny sparkling piece of the universe hanging above her bed.

"I'll just fix that tap, then we'll be off, shall we?" Grandpa climbed down from the stepladder, leaving Jax and Beans still gazing up at the mobile.

It's almost as beautiful as the real thing, Beans commented approvingly.

Jax pictured her little moon kitten hurtling past fiery stars and mysterious unknown planets.

I love Moonbeans but he doesn't belong to me, she thought suddenly. She'd known this for a long time, but now she *felt* it with a real ache inside.

Grandpa popped his head back round the door. "I just thought I'd check that you still want to go to this City Farm or whatever it's called? You wouldn't rather go to the cinema or something?"

Beans fixed her with an imploring golden stare and Jax said quickly, "No, I do, Grandpa. I really, *really* want to go to the City Farm."

The moment Grandpa's car pulled up at the City Farm, Bandit came trotting towards them, making his husky chirruping sound. Jax knew now what he'd been trying to tell her on their class trip. He was telling her he'd located Beans's dad for him.

She had already secretly unfastened her backpack. Now she casually placed it on the ground, pretending to be doing up her jacket. When she picked up her backpack  again, it felt noticeably lighter and Bandit was hurrying into the distance with an invisible Moonbeans, on their way to meet Spangle.

"Good luck, Beans," she whispered.

She turned back to her grandpa, who was inhaling happily. "Now that's a *real* country smell!" he said approvingly. "So where are we going first, Ellie Mae?"

After a couple of hours, Grandpa was ready for a snack and a sit-down. He'd been fascinated by everything but he especially loved the shire horses, as Jax had known he would, plus the mad antics of the puppies had made him laugh out loud.

Outside the farm café, Jax was thrilled to bump into Nan and Simon. It really tickled her when Simon didn't recognize her out of school uniform. (She was wearing her favourite weekend outfit: red velvet shorts with charcoal grey leggings and a fluffy red fleece.) But Nan said, "I remember you! Bandit followed you all around the farm. You were with that red-haired boy who was so good with the animals!"

"I told my mum she has to tell everybody about the City Farm," Jax said, beaming. "You should be getting loads of volunteers soon!"

"That's brilliant. Thanks, Jax!" said Nan. "It seems like the word is finally starting to spread. We're getting a few more bookings for school visits too, aren't we, Simon?"

He nodded but Jax could see that they were still worried.

"Anyway, we're off to a fundraising meeting," Simon said with a sigh. "Wish us luck!"

Soon Jax and her grandpa were sitting at a window table in the visitors' café. Jax blew carefully on her hot chocolate to cool it, as she swung her legs. Nan and Simon were at a nearby table with some other City Farm helpers, and a man with grey hair who Jax guessed must be the City Farm's owner. "That's the most fun I've had since your talent show," Grandpa was saying, chuckling. "It was worth coming just to see those puppies! Just wonderful."

"You should get a puppy, Grandpa," Jax told him. "It would be fun!"

Grandpa shook his head, laughing. "Hard work, more like. Puppies need training."

"A rescue dog, then. There are loads of dogs needing good homes. We could take it for walks at the weekends. I'm serious, Grandpa. You're like Conrad – being around animals makes you happy."

"Wasn't Conrad that boy who was Howard's MC at the talent show?"

Jax sighed. "Yes, I'm really worried about him."

Grandpa listened, nodding, as she told him about Conrad and the school trip and the episode with the mice that had got him into so much trouble.

"I'd like to meet your friend Conrad," he said

when she'd finished. "He seems like an interesting boy."

"He *is*! But because he used to be a bully, everyone thinks he's one of the bad boys. Even his mum," she added unhappily, remembering how Conrad's mum had scolded him on the way out of school."

Just then, Jax felt something soft brush against her ankles. Moonbeans was back.

At the same moment, Grandpa glanced around as the grey-haired man pushed back his chair and stood up. Nan was quickly gathering up a pile of papers. It seemed like the fundraising meeting was over. To Jax's surprise, Grandpa stood up too and cleared his throat. "Excuse me for butting in, but did I hear you say the City Farm is looking for volunteers?"

"Are you offering?" asked the man with grey hair.

"I might be," Grandpa said cautiously.

The man held out his hand. "I'm Bob McCreedy, the farm manager. How much experience do you have with animals?" he asked bluntly.

"I grew up in the country," Grandpa said. "I worked on a farm for most of my school holidays. I suppose you're looking for young volunteers though," he sighed, "not old codgers like me?"

The manager shook his head. "We welcome everybody, old or young, so long as they care about animals and they're willing to work hard."

Old or young! As Bob McCreedy said the words, Jax felt a jolt of magic shoot through her and Moonbeans, and knew that they were both having the same genius idea. It seemed so obvious to her now that she couldn't imagine why they hadn't thought of it before! If it worked, it wouldn't matter that Conrad couldn't have a pet. He'd be able to hang out with animals all day long at the City Farm!

I'm going to ask him, she told Beans silently. She shyly put up her hand. "Could my friend Conrad be a City Farm volunteer?"

Bob McCreedy turned to her, smiling. "How old is your friend?"

"Nine. It's his birthday next week, so he's nearly ten."

"That's rather young for such a big commitment," he said doubtfully. "We'd need to talk to his parents before we could make a decision and even then…"

Beans! Jax said desperately. *I need backup!* This might be their one and only chance to make Conrad's dream come true and she was determined not to waste it.

I'm on it! Beans said at once.

111

The visitors' café
began to fizz and
shimmer as
Moonbeans launched
into the Purr of Power.

"Ask Nan and Simon," Jax pleaded with Mr.
McCreedy. "They saw how much the animals
loved him. And you saw how much Conrad
loved them, didn't you?" Jax appealed to them.
"Remember when that goat was eating his
jumper, and Conrad said it was the happiest
day of his life?"

Nan nodded. "Conrad is quite a special
person," she told Mr. McCreedy.

By this time Jax could feel Moonbeans's
magic fizzing in her fingers and toes. Luckily
nobody else seemed to notice the steady sound
of purring or the hot pink shimmer that filled
the small café. Like Jax, Beans understood that

this was a make-or-break moment and he was giving it everything he'd got.

Bob McCreedy's expression suddenly softened and Jax breathed a sigh of relief. The magic was working. "I've got a suggestion," he said. "We're planning a very special fundraising show here at Halloween. If you'd put some posters up for us, I'll give you some tickets for you and your friends and I'll throw in a couple extra for Conrad and his mum. How does that sound? That way we'll get to meet Conrad, and his mum can see what our farm is about."

Jax was disappointed. She'd hoped that Mr. McCreedy would say he'd take Conrad on then and there, but Grandpa said firmly, "That's an extremely generous offer. Now I think we'll have one last look at those magnificent shire horses, then I'm taking this young lady back home."

And Jax had to leave it at that.

Giving Beans time to hop into her backpack, Jax stood up to follow Grandpa out of the café. As she slung her bag over her shoulders, she just managed to hide her squeak of surprise. *I should have let him cool down after all that purring*, she thought, smirking, as the leftover magic fizzed between her shoulder blades.

By the time Jax and her grandpa had said goodbye to the horses and walked all the way back to the car park, Jax was desperate to know what Beans had found out about his dad. When Grandpa stopped to put his coat in the boot, Jax decided to grab her chance and try to talk to Beans, but just at that moment Nan came running up.

"I've got your free tickets!" she said breathlessly. "Also, Mr. McCreedy said to give you these posters. We want as many Goose

Green people as possible to come along to the show. This is our big chance to put the City Farm on the map and raise some serious funds!"

Grandpa cheerfully took the bundle of posters. "We'll put one up in my daughter's café. Plenty of local people will see it there."

Jax smiled to herself. When Mum moved across the city to Goose Green and took on the café, Grandpa had told her she was making a big mistake. But from the way he'd said "my daughter's café", Jax could tell he was genuinely proud of Mum. It was yet another reason to be grateful to Moonbeans.

"I can't *believe* Spangle doesn't know the name of the circus!"

Jax was keeping her voice down but she wanted to stamp with frustration for Beans.

They had got back just as Mum was closing

the café for the day, and Mum had made everyone delicious cheese-and-ham toasties. Jax had eaten hers, and now she was sitting on the floor in the sitting room, comforting a subdued Moonbeans.

She said she knew the old name. It was called the Amoretti Brothers. But Spangle said that when the circus decided to stop using animals, they decided to change their name as well. She has no idea what they call themselves now.

In the kitchen, Jax heard Grandpa say, "I'd never even heard of city farms until Ellie invited me!"

"And now you might be a City Farm volunteer! Good for you, Dad!" Mum said cheerfully.

"I said you'd put up a couple of posters in the café – I hope you don't mind? They're having a show there at Halloween. They

actually gave us some free tickets." Jax heard
rustling as Grandpa produced the posters.
"I think I'll go too," he added with a chuckle.
"I haven't been to a circus in years."

At the word "circus", Jax instantly scrambled
to her feet and dashed into the kitchen to look
at the flier. As she scanned the curly red and
gold lettering, her eyes grew wide.

The flier showed a
black cat wearing a
miniature version of
a ringmaster's top
hat with stardust
sparkling all around.
The cat in the picture
had one gleaming
white whisker and
enormous golden eyes.

Coming to
Goose Green City Farm
October 31st
for one night only
The
Stardust Circus

It was Moonbeans's dad!

The last-ever mission

8

Jax felt as if she'd been lying awake for hours, watching Grandpa's mobile spinning in the night breeze that came through the open window. Moonbeans had gone to find Rumble and tell him his good news. He'd been out for ages now and her room was getting chilly. Maybe that was why Jax was thinking chilly thoughts…

She knew she should be happy for Moonbeans. He'd been searching for so long, and then suddenly, in just a few days, everything had come together in a big rush.

Now they not only knew the name of his dad's circus, but they'd got free tickets too!

She just hated the feeling that everything could possibly be happening for the last time: the last time she'd hear Beans do his Long-Distance Purr, the last time she'd see her room fizzing with magic.

Not that Moonbeans had said he was leaving. But in exactly one week, The Stardust Circus was coming to Goose Green and Beans would finally meet his dad. Everything was going to change. Jax could feel it, like a ticking clock at the back of her mind, counting off the minutes.

In between feeling sad about Beans, she fretted about their mission to help Conrad. It had been a stroke of luck finding out that the City Farm was open to accepting young volunteers. But they weren't home and dry

– not yet. They still had to get Conrad's mum to the farm to meet Bob McCreedy and the others, plus they had to actually persuade her to let Conrad be a volunteer helper.

Jax thumped her pillow, trying to get comfortable. So many things could go wrong. For starters, Conrad's mum might refuse to accept the free tickets. She might be too busy, or she might not be able to get a babysitter for Conrad's little brothers.

Jax had planned to give the remaining tickets to her other friends. Before Moonbeans came, Jax didn't have a single friend in Goose Green. Now she had loads, all because of a certain little marmalade-coloured moon cat. So it seemed only right that all her friends should be there with her and Beans at The Stardust Circus.

Now Jax had a sudden thought. Suppose she

and her friends got their *own* tickets? Then she could give all the free tickets to Conrad, his mum and his three little brothers? There'd be no need to worry about babysitters!

She heard a familiar soft thud – the sound a small moon cat makes jumping down from a window sill and landing on all four paws. Moonbeans was home, purring the cosy tea-kettle purr that meant he was happy.

Jax hastily pushed all her Conrad worries to the back of her mind. "Was Rumble happy that you'd tracked down your dad?" she asked in her most cheerful voice.

He said if he was a few years younger he'd be chasing his tail!

Jax giggled. "I'd like to see that!"

That's what Claws and the others said!

Moonbeans jumped up beside her and she gave a little shriek. "Your paws are like icicles, Beans!" She cuddled up to him all the same, tightly closing her eyes and refusing to think that, in seven short nights, she could be breathing his jelly-beans smell for the very last time.

Perhaps the Aunts had been talking to Jax in her dreams, because when she opened her eyes the next morning, she was Jax the fighter girl again!

How many nine-year-old girls had been given the chance to go on missions with a magical moon cat? Probably not very many! Instead of feeling sorry for herself, Jax made up her mind to remember how lucky she was.

This could be her last-ever mission, so Ellie Mae Jackson, future world-famous scientist, was going to do everything in her power to make it a REALLY good one.

Beans had gone off somewhere, so Jax decided this was the perfect time to tackle her mum. She found her in the sitting room, still in her PJs, reading the Sunday papers.

Her mum looked up. "Good morning, sweetie. Ready for some breakfast?"

Jax shook her head. "Mum, I really need your help."

"Is it to do with your friend Conrad?" Mum said at once.

Jax blinked in surprise. "How did you know?"

"Grandpa mentioned that you seemed very keen for Conrad to be a City Farm helper. Plus

123

you told me about the mice, remember?"

Jax was relieved. A mind-reading moon cat was bad enough. A mind-reading mum would be too scary for words!

Mum put down her paper. "What can I do for you, sweetie?"

Jax joined her on the sofa. "Mr. McCreedy – he's the manager of the City Farm – gave me some free tickets for the circus," she explained. "He said two were for Conrad and his mum, so that way he can meet them and see if Conrad's mum will let Conrad be a volunteer. But I thought we should probably give *all* the tickets to Conrad's family, otherwise his mum will have to get a babysitter. But that means the rest of us will have to buy our own tickets. But then I wasn't sure if we can actually afford for me to go to the circus? *Can* we, Mum?" Jax finished, slightly out of breath.

Mum looked startled. "Have you been worrying about this all night?"

Jax nodded earnestly.

"Well, we can *definitely* afford to buy you a ticket, so that's one worry out of the way," Mum said, smiling.

"But how will we give the other tickets to Conrad's mum?" Jax asked anxiously. "She might think it's weird if I give them to her."

"You're really on a mission, aren't you?" Mum said, half laughing.

Jax could feel herself going red. Was her mum psychic? "I'm not on a mission. Conrad's my friend, that's all."

Mum gently placed her hand over Jax's. "It's a great idea, Ellie, and I think I can help. Conrad's mum often brings the boys into the café on her day off. I'll just say we've been given more circus tickets than we can use, and would

125

she like to take the boys?"

Jax's face lit up with relief. "That would be brilliant, Mum." Her smile faded. "What if she doesn't come in though?"

Mum gave her a mischievous grin. "The Dream Café is having a special Halloween promotion: if you buy two cupcakes, you get another two free. Everybody in Goose Green will be coming in this week, I promise you!"

Jax sidled closer to her mum and put on her softest, most wheedling voice. "Mum, do you think you could possibly do me one more huge favour?"

Mum was right. On Wednesday after school, Jax ran down to the café with Moonbeans to beg for a free cupcake: double chocolate, her favourite.

(Moonbeans wasn't keen on cake, but he went mad for chocolate icing!) Suddenly the bell gave a soft jangle and Conrad came in with his mum and his three little brothers. Jax pretended to be busy wiping down the counter as her mum picked out all the boys' favourite cakes.

Moonbeans began to weave between the tables and Jax heard him doing the Purr of Power.

"I'm so glad you came in," Mum said, beaming. "I've been given extra tickets for the circus on Saturday. They're handing them out to everyone who puts up some posters. I don't suppose you'd like to take the boys?"

Jax kept on wiping the counter, not daring to breathe, as the air around her grew increasingly fizzy and pink.

Conrad's mum blinked in surprise. "Are you sure?"

Mum nodded. "I'd like them to go to someone who can use them."

"Then I accept!" Conrad's mum said, smiling. "Thank you! I didn't even know the circus was coming. My boys would have totally missed out on a treat!" She looked surprised and pleased as she took her boys over to a spare table. Even Conrad looked a *tiny* bit pleased, Jax noticed.

"Good job," Jax whispered to Beans. She looked around the shimmery café and at her purring moon cat, and forced herself not to think that this might be the very last time.

Jax was just going to bed when Mum came upstairs with the phone. "It's your grandpa. I told him about you giving away all the free tickets."

"He's not cross with me, is he?" Jax said

anxiously. She remembered now that Grandpa had said he wanted to come.

"Talk to him!" Mum said with a grin.

When Jax put the phone down ten minutes later, she was smiling from ear to ear. Grandpa had offered to take Jax and ALL her friends to the circus! He said it was his treat. All her friends would be coming now, just like she'd dreamed!

I'm not going to think about after the circus, Jax thought, fiercely. She was Jax the fighter girl, and she was going to concentrate on her mission – maybe her last-ever mission with Beans.

The Stardust Circus

9

It was the night before Halloween. Somewhere, people were letting off fireworks. Jax stood by her window in her PJs, watching showers of brightly coloured stars shoot up into the darkness.

Whoosh! A rocket went zooming up into the dark, exploding into brilliant green and hot pink flowers that rained back down to earth.

The Stardust Circus would be arriving tonight. Jax seemed to remember that circuses always came in the night – it was one of the things that made them so magical. When

morning came, the gaudy
circus tent and caravans
would just mysteriously be
there in the field, as if
they'd all sprouted up out
of the earth like mushrooms.

She heard the sudden sharp snap of the cat
flap and hastily jumped into bed. Moonbeans
was back. *No gloomy thoughts, Jax*, she scolded
herself.

She heard Beans's paws thundering upstairs
like they had the night he found out about his
dad. He burst into her room. *My dad! What if he
doesn't like me?* His eyes were yellow-gold pools
of fear.

"Oh, Beans!" Jax gathered him into her
arms. She'd never seen him like this before.
"*Everybody* loves you, even dogs, and dogs *hate*
cats! No *way* is your dad not going to love you!"

It turned out that Jax didn't have time for sad and gloomy thoughts. She spent most of her last night with Moonbeans trying to keep him calm, talking about anything that popped into her head – anything at all that might distract him from his panic.

She told him that she thought The Stardust Circus was the perfect name for Mungo's circus. "My dad used to say that everything in the universe was made out of the same stardust. You  and me, Conrad, the Aunts, even my goldfish."

The Aunts say that too. Moonbeans seemed slightly comforted.

She asked him if he had finally told the Aunts about finding his dad and he said he had. *They say they'll be thinking of me.*

Finally Jax sang "Yellow Bird" to him, over

and over. It didn't lull him to sleep but it helped to soothe him. Gradually the sky grew lighter.

"Let's watch the sun come up," she suggested, smothering a yawn. "We watched it on your first day here, remember?"

Jax and her moon cat went over to the window, and waited for the dawn. *Maybe my dad is watching the sunrise too*, he said.

"I love you, Beans," Jax said softly, as the morning light filled the sky.

"Grandpa's here!" Mum called up the stairs a few hours later.

Jax had been dressed and ready for ages, but she suddenly found that she was shaking. She planted a brisk kiss on Moonbeans's nose. "You'll be fine," she told him, swallowing. You'd better jump into my bag and turn invisible now." He jumped into her backpack, shut his eyes, and was gone in a blink.

Jax tried not to think *Last time, last time*, but she just couldn't help it.

On the way to the circus, Grandpa and Lilia were easily the most excited out of everyone in the car; out of all the humans anyway, Jax decided.

Grandpa chatted about a circus he'd been to when he was a boy. His bossy Auntie Linda had insisted on sitting in the front row, but quickly regretted it when a lion backed up to the edge of the cage separating the lions from the audience and did an enormous wee all over her!

"Are you okay?" Howard asked Jax.

"I'm fine," she said quickly. "Why wouldn't I be?"

"It's just that you're not usually this quiet."

Just then, Lilia gasped, "Jax! Look!"

134

She had spotted the
circus tent in one of
the City Farm fields. It
looked magical with its
brightly coloured flags
fluttering in the afternoon sun.

Grandpa parked the car and they went to
join the queue snaking its way towards the big
top. Jax could smell trodden grass and diesel
from the generator and knew that Beans could
smell it too.

We're here, she told him silently. *I'm going to
let you out now.*

Jax glanced furtively in the direction of the
circus people's caravans, but there was nothing
to see except lines of washing flapping in the
breeze.

Ruby-Rose caught her looking. "What's up?
You're really jumpy."

Jax ignored her. She was looking out for Bandit, the farm cat. Rumble had sent a message telling him to take Moonbeans to meet his dad. All at once, Bandit emerged from behind a loudly humming generator.

"*Ow!*" Jax said in a loud voice. "I've got a stone in my shoe!" She quickly crouched down, putting her bag on the ground. She felt an invisible tail brush past as Moonbeans bounded away and felt a terrible pang. *I didn't even say a proper goodbye*, she thought.

"Come on, we want to get good seats," Grandpa grumbled.

The queue was much shorter now and Jax and her friends were soon following Grandpa into the big top. But at the last minute Jax paused. "Save me a seat, okay!" she gabbled.

She flew out of the tent, feeling as if she was being pulled by an invisible string, past the noisy generator, jumping over loops of electrical cable. She had to have one last glimpse of Moonbeans. She had to know that he was all right.

Suddenly she stopped, breathing fast. On the top step of the very last caravan, a glossy black cat sat calmly washing. His single white whisker gleamed in the sunlight.

She was looking for Moonbeans. But she'd found Mungo.

He was every bit as handsome as Spangle had said. Spangle had told Beans that Mungo didn't perform with the circus, but he was like their lucky mascot, and now that he was right in front of her, Jax could see why.

Bandit came stalking into view, his tail

waving, looking more like a pirate cat than ever. He mewed encouragingly to someone Jax couldn't see. There was a bright pink shimmer and Moonbeans suddenly appeared beside him.

Jax felt her heart give a painful thump as the large black cat and the small alien kitten gazed at each other. Mungo slowly strolled up to Beans and sniffed him all over. Jax wondered if he could smell the jelly-beans smell that had followed Beans all the way from a strange little planet with five moons. To her amazement and relief, Mungo gave his son's ear a rough but loving lick. They walked off together, their tails waving like banners, and Jax heard the unmistakable sound of two cats purring.

"Goodbye, Beans," she whispered.

"Are you okay?" Howard had come to look for her.

"I just…lost something. I'm coming now."

"That little circus cat looks just like your Moonbeans," Howard commented.

"I know," Jax said, swallowing.

It's hard to be sad at the circus and Jax couldn't help being caught up in the excitement. The name, The Stardust Circus, should have given her a clue, but Jax hadn't expected the big top to be hung all over with sparkling stars that gave out musical chimes any time they were touched. It was absolutely the perfect circus for Jax, because everything was about space.

Instead of a comical, battered old car, the clowns arrived in a rusty old rocket that pumped out clouds of purple smoke. They looked astonished to find a handwritten sign saying *The Moon* in the middle of the circus ring, and immediately tried to plant a flag, which kept falling down.

Something was
wrong with
their rocket
too, so the
clowns rushed
around trying to fix it,
tripping over each other and pouring in
buckets of water that turned out to be glitter.
Like always with clowns, the harder they tried
to mend it, the more their ship fell to pieces.
At last they climbed back into what was left
of their spacecraft and, to cheers from the
audience, they went pedalling crazily out of
the big top.

Howard hooted with laughter along with
all the others, but he couldn't help telling Jax
solemnly, "The glitter would really float
upwards! There's no gravity on the moon."

Jax saw Conrad and his brothers laughing

and clapping in a row near the front. Mr. McCreedy was in the row behind them with Nan and Simon, and Jax noticed Nan pointing Conrad out to him.

There were no lions, elephants or circus ponies at The Stardust Circus, but there were lightning-fast jugglers, bare-chested fire-eaters, and fearless  acrobats, who threw each other around as if they were made out of rubber.

The last act was the best. Strange music filled the air and all around the tent there were sounds of explosions and brilliant bursts of light, as if new stars and planets were being born far out in space.

Eerie-looking figures ran on, their faces painted silver and gold. Their costumes glittered as if they'd been sprinkled with frost.

Jax instantly figured out what they were. "They're the solar system!" she whispered to Grandpa. "The boy with the moons on his headdress is Neptune, the glittery gold one is the sun, the fiery red one is Mars, and the little girl with the crown of berries is Planet Earth."

One by one, the strange glittering figures swarmed up to a dizzy platform high above the ring. They took it in turns to dangle from swings, swooping under and over each other like fabulous birds. Then they unfurled sparkling ropes, using them to swing out further and still further from the platform.

When each planet was in his or her proper position, they began to spin faster and faster, until all Jax could see was a glittering blur. Even the little girl who was Planet Earth was spinning, though she wasn't as high as the others, and there was a safety net underneath all the performers.

As the planets kept spinning, the tent erupted with fabulous firework effects. Conrad's baby brother's eyes went huge but he didn't cry. He just stretched out his arms and laughed and laughed. Jax saw Conrad's mum saying something to Conrad that made him smile.

 And then it was all over. Beans had said Conrad needed more magic in his life, and The Stardust Circus was *totally* magic. Jax felt like she'd been on an exhausting journey across the universe and back.

But she couldn't afford to relax, not yet.
She still had a job to do for the Aunts, and since
Moonbeans wasn't there, it was down to Jax to
complete their mission.

"Just a sec," she told Grandpa, as they rose
from their seats. She pushed her way through
the crowd till she reached Nan, Simon and
Mr. McCreedy. "Hi," she said shyly. "My mum
says you're all invited back to her café. You too,"
she told Conrad's family. "You've got to come,"
she whispered to Conrad. "Mum's got a special
surprise."

Halloween had come to the Dream Café!

Mum, Nadia and Lexie, their Saturday girl,
had been really busy, Jax thought. Grinning
Halloween pumpkins and toothy sugar skulls
glimmered in the windows of the café. Inside,
spooky bats and spiders hung from the ceiling,

and the tables were spread
with Nadia's gruesome
Halloween goodies.

"Did Nadia make that
'favour' I asked you about?" Jax whispered to
her mum.

"She brought it over after you and Grandpa
left," Mum whispered back. "Let me know when
you want me to switch off the lights."

Luckily Conrad and his family arrived at the
same time as the City Farm people. This made
Jax's job much easier.

Jax and her mum met them at the door and
led them to their large table. "You're all our
guests of honour," Jax explained.

Mr. McCreedy was looking around the café
with a baffled expression. "This place has such
a magical atmosphere!"

"Everyone says that," said Jax's mum, smiling.

Would it feel so magical tomorrow, though? Jax wondered. How long would it take for Moonbeans's magic to wear off now that he was gone? But she couldn't think about that now, because it was time to give her mum the special signal.

The lights dimmed and Lexie appeared from the kitchen, carefully carrying a huge cake with ten lighted candles.

Conrad's eyes grew wide. "That isn't for me?" he faltered.

"It's *totally* for you," Jax told him, smiling, as everybody in the café started singing "Happy Birthday" to an astonished Conrad.

"I know it's not your birthday till next week," Jax said, "but we've organized you a surprise present – haven't we, Mr. McCreedy?" She gave him a meaningful stare and he quickly nodded.

"I've been hearing how brilliant you are with animals, Conrad," Mr. McCreedy said. "So, if your mum agrees, we'd like you to come to the City Farm on Saturdays to help out with the animals as a volunteer."

Conrad's mum looked doubtful. "Conrad has always been keen on animals," she admitted. "But I don't know if—"

Jax held her breath. Without Moonbeans to save the situation with his Purr of Power, she knew their mission could still go horribly wrong.

"I'm thinking of being a volunteer myself," Grandpa called over from the next table. "So if transport is a problem, Conrad can come with me."

Conrad's mum gave a startled smile. "If it wouldn't put you to too much trouble," she said. "With their dad working so much, I never have a spare moment."

"It would be my pleasure," Grandpa said gruffly. "Besides, I think Conrad and I may be kindred spirits!" He grinned at Conrad, who looked as if he thought he was dreaming.

"Well, in that case, I'm sure Conrad would jump at the chance to be a volunteer, wouldn't you, Conrad?" said his mum.

Conrad himself still hadn't uttered a word, but an amazed smile was spreading across his face.

"Make a speech!" Ruby-Rose shouted at him.

Jax had to blink hard. Their plan had worked out perfectly, yet she was fighting back tears. Though she had been telling herself all day that Moonbeans wasn't coming back, a tiny part of her had hoped that the little moon cat would find a way to be with her to see the successful conclusion of their mission. But now their mission had been completed and, although she knew she should be happy for Conrad, all she could think was that Beans still hadn't showed up. So now she absolutely *knew* that he wasn't ever coming back.

Ruby-Rose was still yelling, "Speech!"

At last Conrad stood up, blushing furiously. "I might talk a lot, but I'm no good at speeches, so I'm just going to say thanks for everything! This is, like, the best present ever!" And he sat down again, absolutely scarlet in the face. "This *is* really happening, isn't it?" he whispered to Jax.

She just nodded and did her best to smile. *Yes, it's really happening, Conrad*, she told him silently, with an aching heart. *This is the Dream Café, where dreams come true.*

Did Moonbeans know their mission was successful? Could her little moon cat still read her mind, even from far away? Jax really hoped that he could.

"Are you coming trick-or-treating with us, Conrad?" Lilia asked him shyly.

"Try and stop me!" he said, grinning.

"You'd better go and get changed then," Ruby-Rose told him bossily. "We'll all meet up back here in half an hour."

Jax had forgotten all about going trick-or-treating and wished she didn't have to go. But her friends would think it was strange if she told them to go without her. She trailed slowly upstairs to find her special 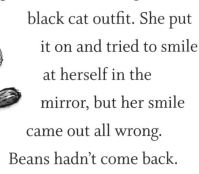 black cat outfit. She put it on and tried to smile at herself in the mirror, but her smile came out all wrong.

Beans hadn't come back. Tonight the circus would be packing up and Moonbeans would be going with them, just as she'd dreaded. When Jax came back from going trick-or-treating with her friends, her room would be empty: no jelly-beans smell, no magic pink shimmer, just a lonely little goldfish swimming up and down in his tank.

It would be like nothing had ever happened. It would be like she'd just imagined the whole thing. Jax didn't think she could be a fighter girl any more. It hurt too much. She threw herself on her bed and burst into tears.

Don't cry.

Jax sat up again with a gasp. Moonbeans was in the doorway. She could see the moon sparkles in his fur glinting in the light from the landing.

For a moment, she was too stunned to speak. "I thought you weren't coming back," she whispered. She swallowed hard as it dawned on her why he'd come. "Did you just come back to say goodbye?"

The little cat seemed bewildered. *Goodbye? I'm not going anywhere. You're my human.*

"I thought you'd gone with the circus," she quavered. "I thought you'd want to stay with your dad."

He came to wind around her legs. *The circus is my dad's life, not mine,* he said calmly. *Besides, we've got all this work to do for the Aunts. Things worked out fine for Conrad – good job, by the way! – but there are still hundreds and thousands of dreams in Goose Green waiting to come true. Anyway,* he added slyly, *you said you'd take me out trick-or-treating!*

Suddenly Jax was laughing and crying all at the same time. "Okay, you bossy little moon cat! At least let me finish getting dressed!" Sniffing back the last of her tears, she put on her furry pussycat ears and her glow-in-the-dark bangles, and last of all she picked up her trick-or-treat bag. "Are you ready for the spookiest night of the year?"

I'm ready, he told her.

Jax couldn't help letting out a shriek when she saw the terrifying creatures that were waiting for them downstairs in the hall: a zombie with a bloodstained rubber knife through his head, a vampire with fangs, a white-faced ghost in a cloak, and a girl werewolf. She knew, really, that they were her friends, Howard, Conrad, Lilia and Ruby-Rose, but they still gave her a fright.

She called goodbye to her mum and they went off, laughing and chatting.

"Trick or treat!" they shouted outside the

Red Hot Wok, and Mei Lee came out with a bag of sweets for them to share.

Jax felt Beans brush against her leggings. His eyes glowed in the dark like amber flames. *Wait till I tell the Aunts about Halloween!*

"What will you tell them?" she whispered.

I'll tell them that for one night every year, Goose Green is every bit as magic as the planet with five moons!

Jax looked around at all the children wearing wild and wonderful costumes and carrying flickering torches and lanterns as they went from house to house. She thought of the street cats passing messages from one end of Goose Green to the other, and the ripples of magic that were spreading further and further across the city with every mission.

Finally she looked back at the Dream Café, with its windows full of grinning lighted

pumpkins – a magical café where a little girl
lived with her very own moon cat. *Every day is
magic with Moonbeans!* she thought.

Then Conrad tweaked her furry cat ears and
Jax, Beans and their friends went racing off
down the street shouting, "Trick or treat! Trick
or treat!"

A message from Annie

Dear Readers,

Like Ellie Mae Jackson I lived just with my mum. She didn't run a café that sold magical cupcakes, she went out to work as a secretary, and in the holidays I took care of myself most days. I was often lonely and longed for a pet.

One day, most unusually, my mum took a day off from her job and even more unusually she walked me to my village school. She said she had arranged to meet one of my teachers but didn't explain why. Unlike most country people in those days, this teacher owned a car. We waited patiently outside the school gates and eventually saw him driving very carefully along the road. He stopped in front of us and I was amazed to see a tiny but extremely confident tabby kitten riding in the passenger seat. I was even more amazed when my mum explained that this kitten was for me!

I called him Tinker and he was the next best thing to a magical moon cat. He adored me from the start and when he grew older often tried to follow me to school. He seemed to know what time I'd be coming home and was always waiting for me on the corner. I shared all my thoughts and worries with Tinker, just like Jax does with Moonbeans, and I was absolutely convinced that he understood everything I was telling him. Like Moonbeans, Tinker often had to go out roaming on private cat business. Then, during the night he would jump in through my bedroom window, smelling of earth and wild flowers, and curl up with me until morning. I have known dozens of wonderful cats and kittens since then but none of them have been quite as magical and special as Tinker...except Beans. I hope you'll love my magical moon cat as much as I do.

Love and moon dust,
Annie xxx

www.anniedaltonwriter.co.uk

More deliciously delectable recipes
★ from THE DREAM CAFÉ ★

Banana Buns

We all know Conrad is a cheeky monkey, so it's no surprise that these banana buns are his favourite after-school snack. Try to use the ripest bananas you can find to guarantee a super-juicy flavour. To make these treats dairy-free, swap the cream cheese frosting for glacé icing, and use dairy-free spread – easy!

FOR THE BUNS (makes 12)

You will need:

125g (4½oz) softened butter or soft margarine

150g (5oz) soft dark brown sugar

2 large eggs

1 teaspoon of vanilla essence

4 large, ripe bananas

250g (9oz) self-raising flour

½ teaspoon of baking powder

1 teaspoon of lemon juice

FOR THE CREAM CHEESE FROSTING

You wil need:

50g (2oz) icing sugar

200g (7oz) full-fat cream cheese, at room temperature

1 tablespoon of lemon juice

1. Heat the oven to 180°C / Gas mark 4. Fill the tray with paper cases.

2. Put the butter and sugar in a big bowl. Beat them together until the mixture is pale and fluffy.

3. Break an egg into a cup, then put it in a small bowl. Do the same with the other egg. Add the vanilla essence. Mix with a fork.

4. Put a spoonful of the egg in the big bowl. Beat it in well. Add the rest of the egg, a spoonful at a time, beating well each time.

5. Peel the bananas and put them in a bowl. Mash them with a fork or potato masher. Mix in the lemon juice. Tip the mixture into the big bowl and mix it in.

6. Sift the flour and baking powder over the mixture. Mix it in well.

7. Spoon the mixture into the cases. Bake for 20-25 minutes, or until browned and firm.

8. Leave the cakes for 5 minutes, then put them on a wire rack and leave them to cool.

9. Now it's time to make the cream cheese frosting. Sift the icing sugar into a large bowl and add the cream cheese and lemon juice. Mix gently.

10. Spread the frosting over the cakes. You can even decorate them with slices of fresh banana or walnut pieces.

DAIRY-FREE OPTION

For a dairy-free topping, grab some glacé icing. Sift 175g (6oz) icing sugar into a bowl, and mix with 1½ tablespoons of warm water. Add food colouring for a party feel.

Honey Spice Cakes
contains nuts!

It's cool, crunchy-leaf time in Goose Green, which means it's autumn. Wrap up warm and enjoy these spicy honey cakes around your bonfires. They'll create happy fireworks in your tummy.

FOR THE CAKES (makes about 12-15 squares)

You will need:

1 lemon

1 orange

150g (5oz) soft light brown sugar

150g (5oz) softened butter or soft margarine

3 medium eggs

2 teaspoons of baking powder

150g (5oz) semolina or fine cornmeal (polenta)

2 teaspoons of ground cinnamon

½ teaspoon of ground allspice

150g (5oz) ground almonds

4 tablespoons of runny honey

You will also need a 27 x 18cm (11 x 7in) cake tray.

TO DECORATE (optional)
You will need:
Ready-to-roll icing or white marzipan
Food colouring
Extra honey

1. Heat the oven to 180°C / Gas mark 4. Grease and line the tray.

2. Squeeze the juice from the orange and lemon. Put it in a jug.

3. Put the sugar and butter or margarine in a big bowl. Beat until you have a pale and fluffy mixture.

4. Break an egg into a bowl and beat it. Stir it into the mixture in the big bowl. Do the same with the other eggs. Don't worry if it looks lumpy.

5. Put the baking powder, semolina or cornmeal, cinnamon, allspice and ground almonds in a bowl and mix. Tip them into the large bowl.

6. Add 4 tablespoons of juice from the jug and stir. Scrape the mixture into the tray and level the top with the back of a spoon. Bake for 30-35 minutes.

7. Meanwhile, put the honey in the jug and mix it in. Don't worry if it doesn't all mix in. When the cake is risen and firm, take it out of the oven.

8. Give the mixture in the jug a stir, then pour it over the cake. Leave the cake in the tray to cool, then cut it into 12-15 squares.

FANCY SOME CUPCAKES?

For honey spice cupcakes, heat the oven to 200°C / Gas mark 6 instead. Line a 12-hole deep muffin tray with 12 paper cases. Follow steps 2-6, but spoon the mixture into the cases, baking for 15-20 minutes. Follow the rest of the steps and there you have it – sticky, spicy, honey cupcakes.

* Use cornmeal instead of semolina to make these yummy cakes wheat- and gluten-free. To make them dairy-free, just use dairy-free spread.

LET'S DECORATE!

Why not take some tips from Nadia's amazing Halloween cakes and decorate your treats using ready-to-roll icing or white marzipan? Just follow these top decorating tips!

RAINBOW ICING or MULTI-COLOURED MARZIPAN

* For jazzy cake decorations, just take a golf-ball sized blob of icing or white marzipan and put it in a bowl. Make a hollow in the middle and drop in 1 or 2 drops of food colouring.

* Fold the marzipan or icing over the colouring. Keep folding and squashing it until the colour is evenly mixed through.

CUTTING DECORATIONS

* Dust a surface and rolling pin with icing sugar. Roll out the ready-to-roll icing or marzipan until it is half as thin as your little finger.

* Use mini cookie cutters to cut out shapes. Squeeze the scraps together and roll them out to make more shapes.

MOULDING DECORATIONS

* To make balls, roll a piece of marzipan or ready-to-roll icing between the palms of your hands.

* To press dots or stripes into your ready-to-roll icing or marzipan, press the end or side of a cocktail stick into it.

* To make a cute button shape, cut a circle the size of a button. Press a clean, new button onto it. Remove the button and – ta-da!

* Stick your decorations on the cake using a dab of honey.
* Don't forget! Marzipan contains NUTS.

Whoopie Pies

The name for whoopie pies is supposed to have come about because people loved eating them so much they shouted "whoopie!" This makes them the perfect celebration treat – and Jax has plenty to celebrate. The mission to help Conrad has been a success, Beans has met his dad, and best of all, her magical moon cat is here to stay! Whoopie!

FOR THE PIES (makes about 12 pairs)

You will need:

75g (3oz) butter

1 large egg

150g (5oz) caster sugar

150ml (¼pint) carton of soured cream

2 teaspoons of vanilla essence

3 tablespoons of milk

275g (10oz) plain flour

¾ teaspoon of bicarbonate of soda

FOR THE BUTTERCREAM FILLING

You will need:

50g (2oz) butter, softened

100g (4oz) icing sugar

1 teaspoon of vanilla essence

1. Heat the oven to 180°C / Gas mark 4. Line 2 large baking trays with baking parchment.

2. Put the butter in a small pan. Heat gently until the butter just melts. Take it off the heat.

3. Break the egg into a big bowl. Add the sugar. Whisk for 2-3 minutes, until the mixture is thick and pale.

4. Add the melted butter, soured cream, vanilla and milk. Mix them in gently using a big metal spoon, moving it in the shape of an 8.

5. Sift the flour and bicarbonate of soda over the mixture. Stir them in gently.

6. Put heaped teaspoons of the mixture on the trays, making sure the blobs are well spaced out. Bake for 10-12 minutes, or until golden and just firm.

7. Leave on the trays for 5 minutes, Then, put them on a wire rack to cool.

8. Now make the buttercream. Put the butter in a large mixing bowl and beat with a wooden spoon until it becomes soft and fluffy.

9. Sift one third of the icing sugar into the bowl and stir it in. Then, sift the rest of the icing sugar over the mixture.

10. Add the vanilla. Beat quickly, until you have a pale and fluffy mixture.

11. Spread some on the flat side of the sponge. Gently press another one on top. Make more pies in the same way.

FOR CHOCOLATE WHOOPIE PIES

At step 5, use just 225g (8oz) flour and put 50g (2oz) of cocoa powder in the sieve at the same time.

TO DECORATE YOUR PIES

* Roll a pie over a plate of chocolate drops or sugar sprinkles so all the buttercream becomes dotted with multi-coloured sweets.

* Or if you're nuts for nuts, roll your pie over some chopped nuts.

* Use food colouring to tint your buttercream for a real party feel.

* Drizzle melted chocolate over your pies for an extra-special treat.

YOU CAN FIND ALL THESE **YUMMY** RECIPES,
PLUS **LOADS** MORE IN

OUT NOW!

ISBN: 9781409523369

Fancy finding out some dreamy cake decorating tips?

Or are you a creative kitten in need of a Magical Moon Cat colouring sheet?

BLAST OFF to

www.magicalmooncat.com

Jax and Beans are waiting!

My Magical Moon Cat Page

Hey everyone – it's Jax again. I hope you've loved reading about my adventures with Beans. Now it's time for you to get busy with your own top-secret plans!

Turn your dreams into reality by planning your missions here...

Spice up this page with your fave Moonbeans stickers!

Jot down your
yummiest cake recipes here!

Or get creative
with some
space-inspired
doodles

Magical Moon Cat

Join Jax and Moonbeans and collect
every magical mission!

Moonbeans and the Dream Café

Jax is lonely since moving house to follow Mum's dream of
opening a cool café. But then a sparkly pink lightning bolt
delivers a cute alien kitten to Jax's home, and it looks like
her luck is about to change!

ISBN: 9781409526315

Moonbeans and the Shining Star

When Moonbeans announces he's on a mission to cheer
up stroppy starlet, Ruby-Rose, Jax is dismayed. Ruby-Rose
thinks she's the bee's knees because she goes to stage
school. But is it just an act?

ISBN: 9781409526322

Moonbeans and the Talent Show

Hubble, the white rabbit, is worried about his owner,
Howard. He dreams of performing a dazzling magic act
in the school talent show, but his act has more mishaps
than magic. Can Jax and Beans help Howard shine?

ISBN: 9781409526339

If you loved Moonbeans, check out ☆

Amy Wild, Animal Talker
by Diana Kimpton

☆

The Secret Necklace ISBN 9781409504290
Amy is thrilled to discover she can talk to animals!
But making friends is harder than she thought...

The Musical Mouse ISBN 9781409504306
There's a singing mouse at school! Can Amy find it
a new home before the headmaster catches it?

☆

The Mystery Cat ISBN 9781409504313
Amy has to track down the owners of a playful ginger
cat who's lost his home...and his memory.

The Great Sheep Race ISBN 9781409504337
Will Amy train the Island's sheep in time for her
school fair's big fundraiser – a Great Sheep Race?

☆

The Furry Detectives ISBN 9781409504320
Things have been going missing on the Island and
Amy suspects there's an animal thief at work...

☆

The Star-Struck Parrot ISBN 9781409504344
Amy gets to be an extra in a film shot on the Island...
but can she help Plato the parrot land a part too?

The Lost Treasure ISBN 9781409521037
An ancient ring is discovered on the Island, sparking
a hunt for buried treasure...and causing chaos.

☆

The Vanishing Cat ISBN 9781409521044
When one of the animals in the clan goes missing,
Amy faces her biggest mystery yet...

For more tales of magic and friendship,
zoom to
www.fiction.usborne.com